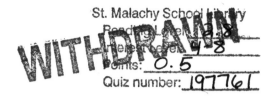

POWER CODERS

THE CHATBOT MYSTERY

C.R. MCKAY

ILLUSTRATED BY JOEL GENNARI

PowerKiDS
press™

New York

Published in 2019 by The Rosen Publishing Group, Inc.
29 East 21st Street, New York, NY 10010

First Edition

Illustrator: Joel Gennari
Interior Layout: Tanya Dellaccio
Managing Editor: Nathalie Beullens-Maoui
Editorial Director: Greg Roza

Library of Congress Cataloging-in-Publication Data

Names: McKay, C. R.
Title: The chatbot mystery / C.R. McKay.
Description: New York : PowerKids Press, [2019] | Series: Power Coders |
Identifiers: LCCN 2017060371| ISBN 9781538340097 (library bound) | ISBN
   9781538340103 (pbk.) | ISBN 9781538340110 (6 pack)
Subjects: | CYAC: Application software–Fiction. | Computer
   programming–Fiction. | Friendship–Fiction.
Classification: LCC PZ7.1.M43543 Ch 2018 | DDC [Fic]–dc23
LC record available at https://lccn.loc.gov/2017060371

Manufactured in the United States of America

CPSIA Compliance Information: Batch CS18PK: For Further Information contact Rosen Publishing, New York, New York at 1-800-237-9932

CONTENTS

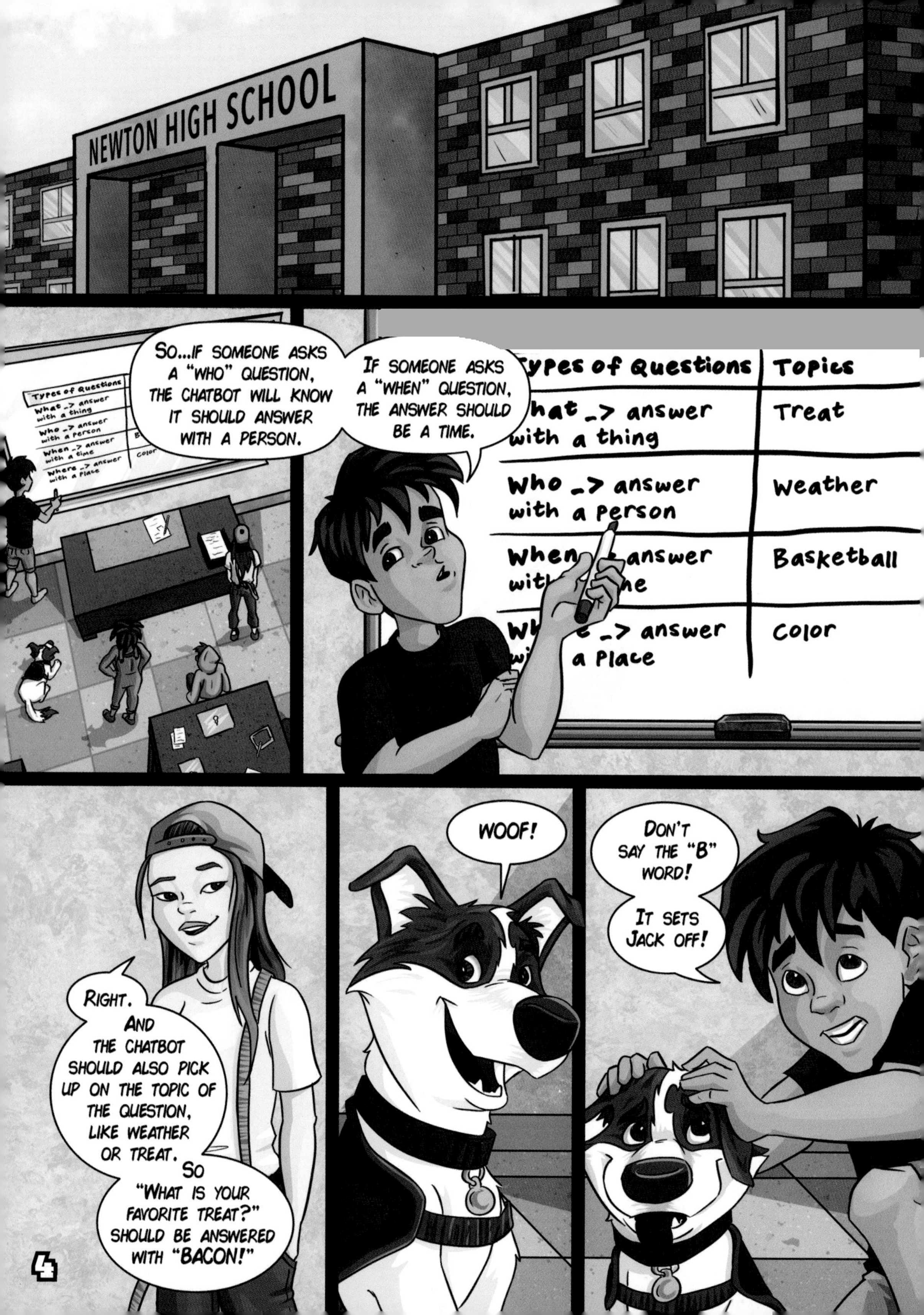
NEWTON HIGH SCHOOL
So...if someone asks a "who" question, the chatbot will know it should answer with a person.
If someone asks a "when" question, the answer should be a time.
ypes of Questions
Topics
hat _> answer with a thing
Treat
Who _> answer with a person
Weather
When
answer
wit
ne
Basketball
Wh
e _> answer
a Place
Color
Right.
And the chatbot should also pick up on the topic of the question, like weather or treat.
So "What is your favorite treat?" should be answered with "Bacon!"
WOOF!
Don't say the "B" word!
It sets Jack off!

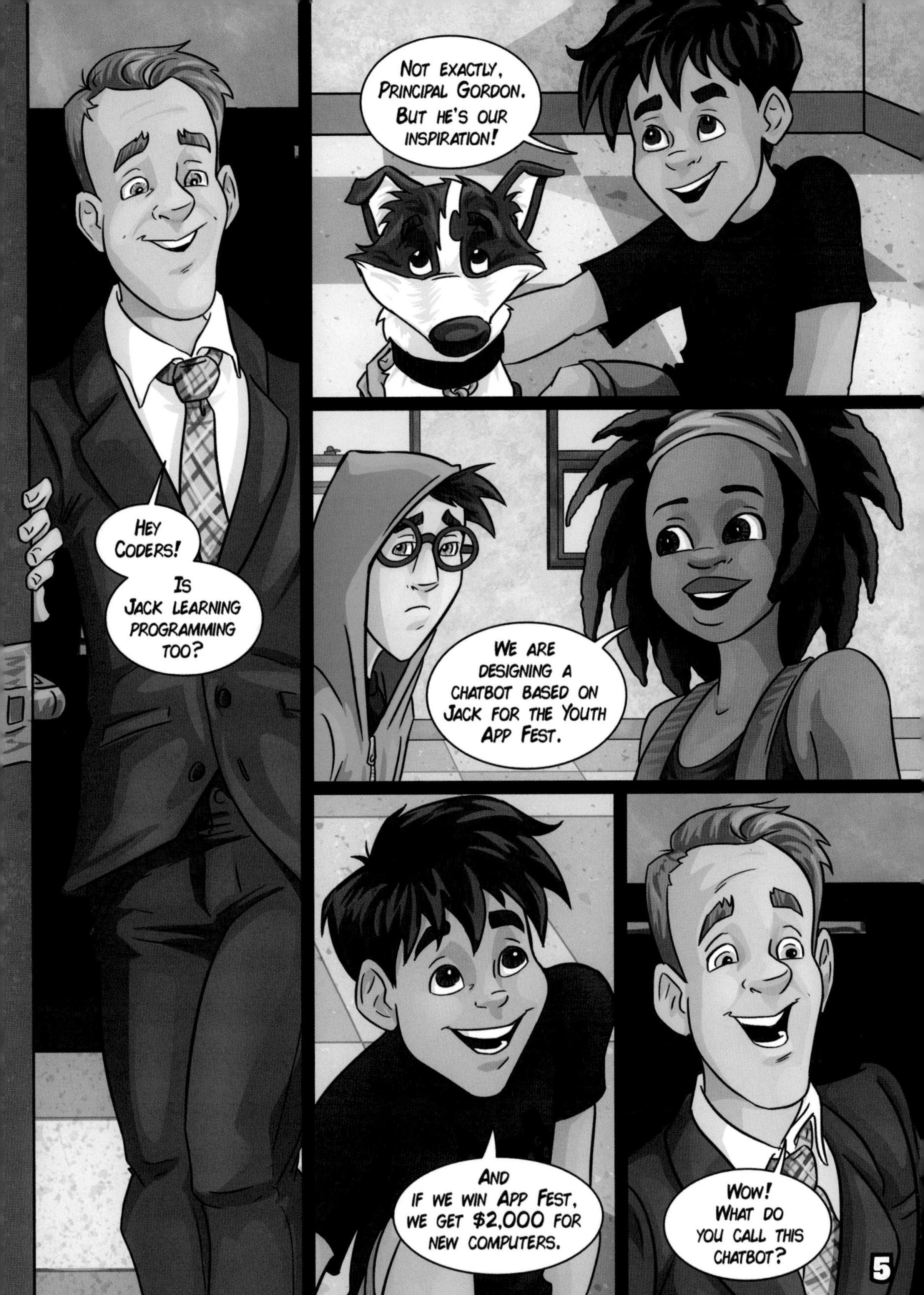
Hey Coders!
Is Jack learning programming too?
Not exactly, Principal Gordon. But he's our inspiration!
We are designing a chatbot based on Jack for the Youth App Fest.
And if we win App Fest, we get $2,000 for new computers.
Wow! What do you call this chatbot?

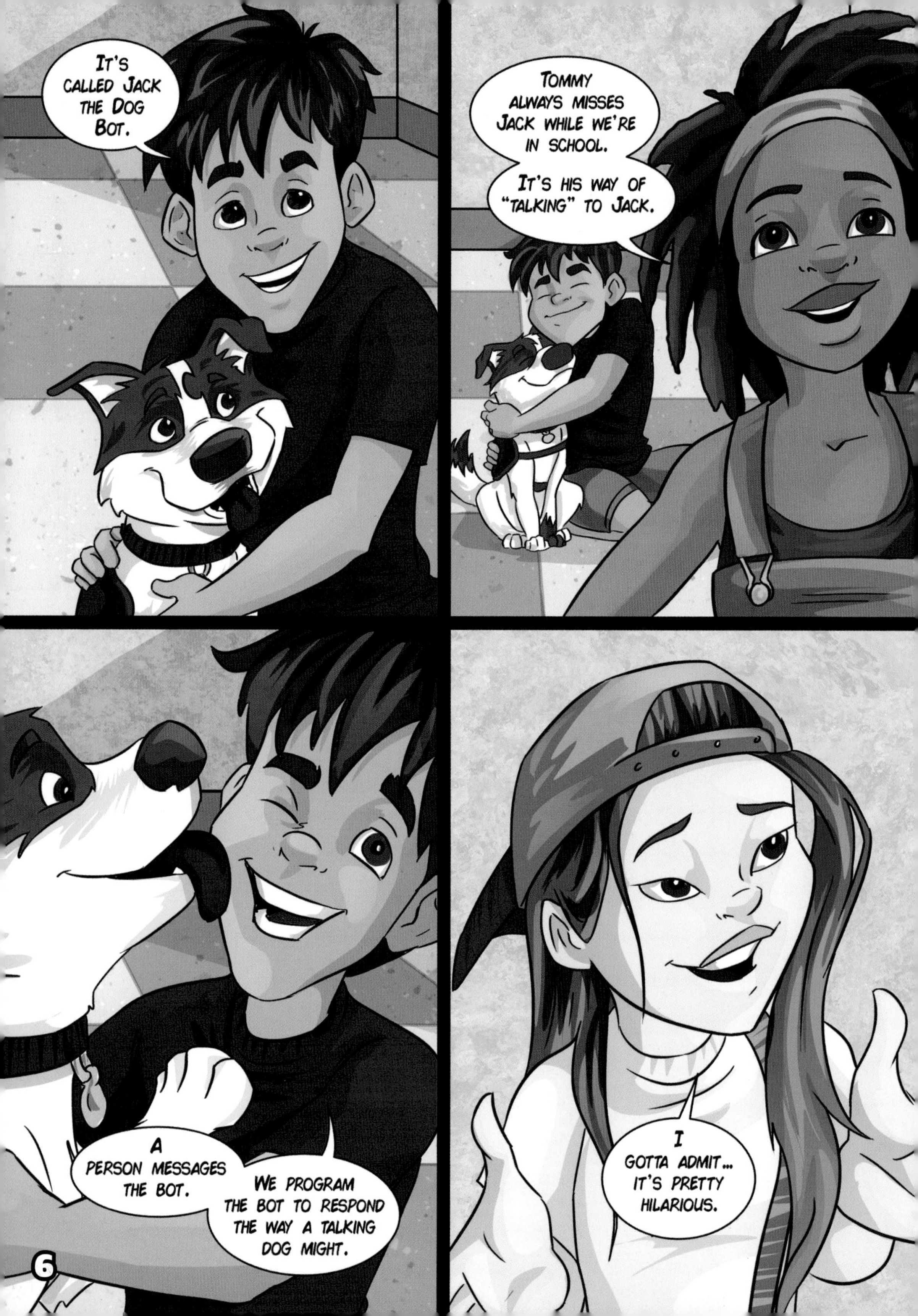
IT'S CALLED JACK THE DOG BOT.
TOMMY ALWAYS MISSES JACK WHILE WE'RE IN SCHOOL.
IT'S HIS WAY OF "TALKING" TO JACK.
A PERSON MESSAGES THE BOT.
WE PROGRAM THE BOT TO RESPOND THE WAY A TALKING DOG MIGHT.
I GOTTA ADMIT... IT'S PRETTY HILARIOUS.

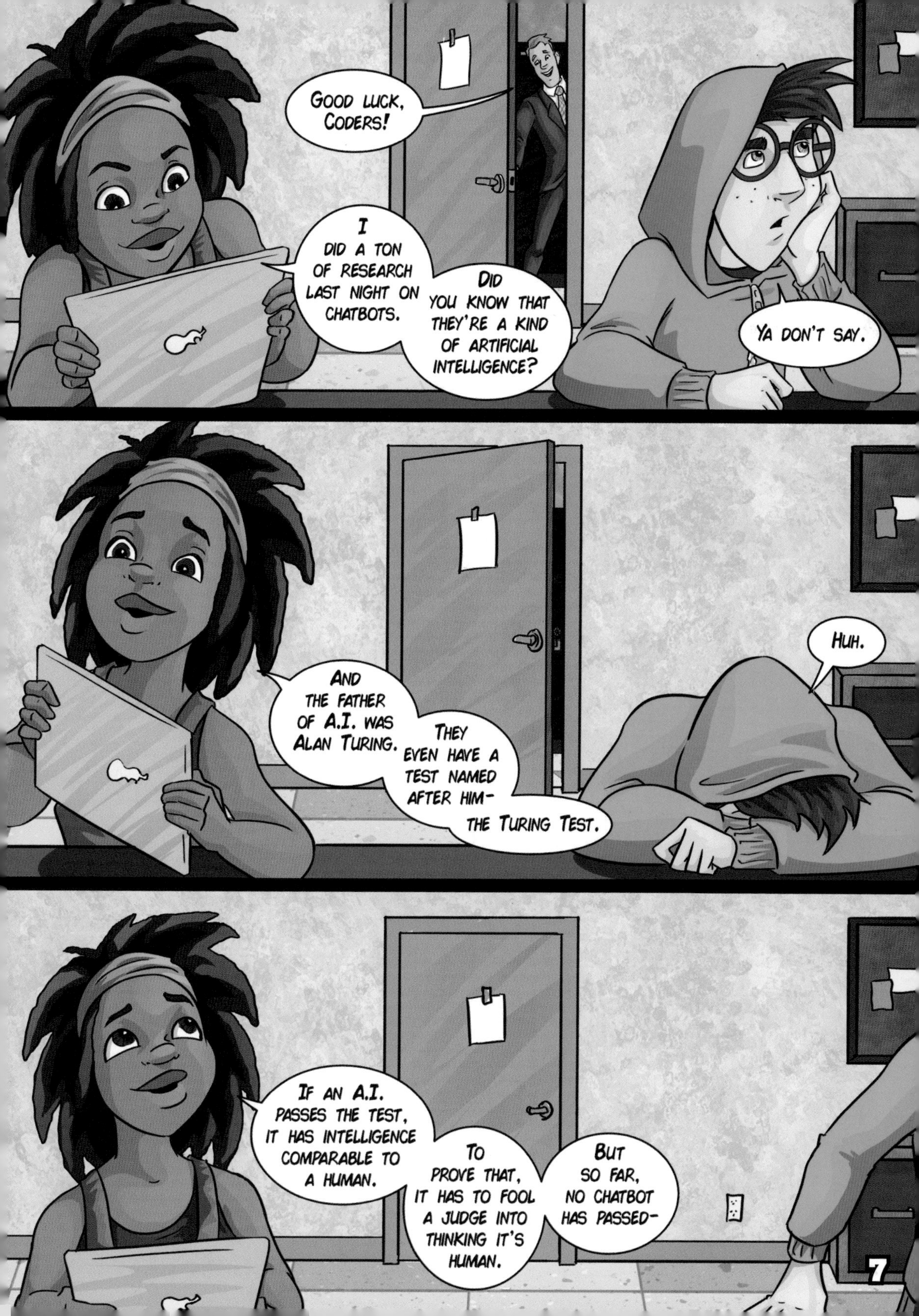
GOOD LUCK, CODERS!
I DID A TON OF RESEARCH LAST NIGHT ON CHATBOTS.
DID YOU KNOW THAT THEY'RE A KIND OF ARTIFICIAL INTELLIGENCE?
YA DON'T SAY.
AND THE FATHER OF A.I. WAS ALAN TURING.
THEY EVEN HAVE A TEST NAMED AFTER HIM-
THE TURING TEST.
HUH.
IF AN A.I. PASSES THE TEST, IT HAS INTELLIGENCE COMPARABLE TO A HUMAN.
TO PROVE THAT, IT HAS TO FOOL A JUDGE INTO THINKING IT'S HUMAN.
BUT SO FAR, NO CHATBOT HAS PASSED-

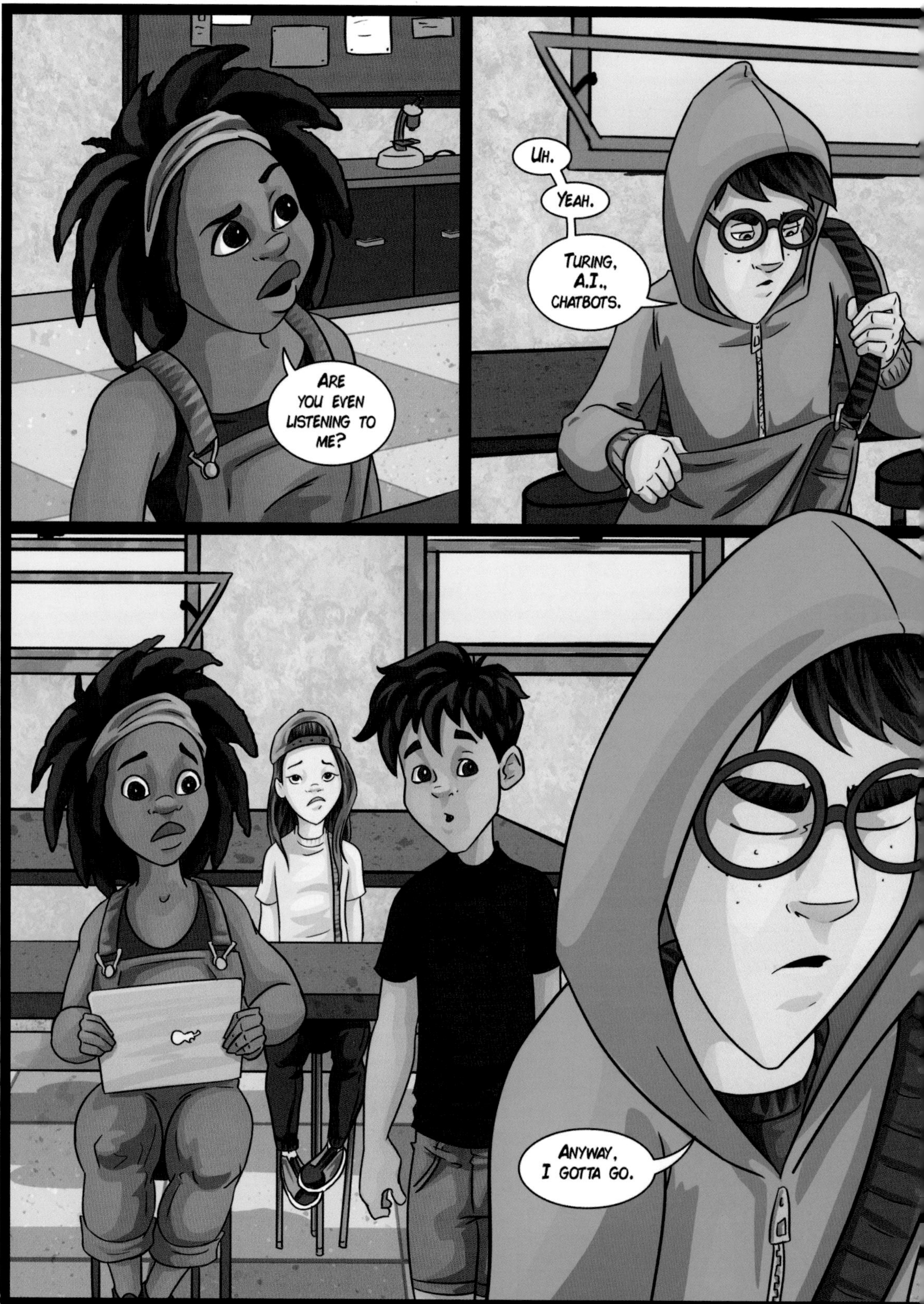
ARE YOU EVEN LISTENING TO ME?
UH.
YEAH.
TURING, A.I., CHATBOTS.
ANYWAY, I GOTTA GO.

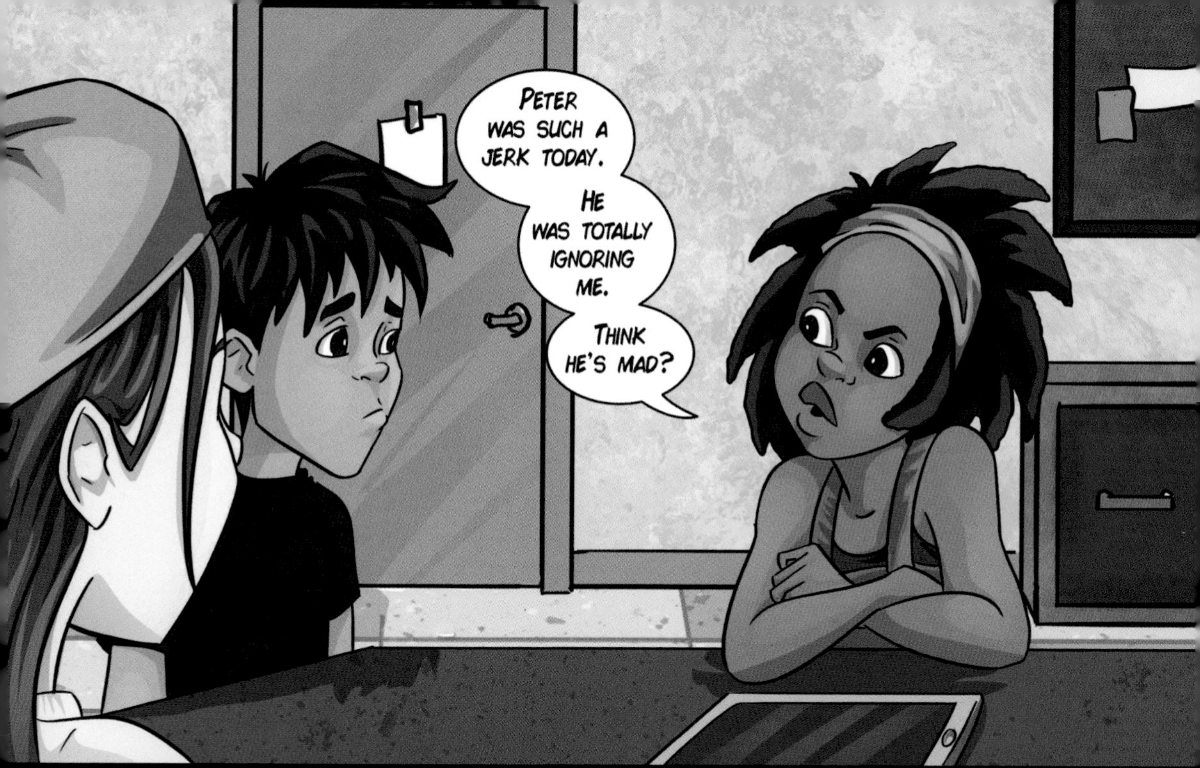
PETER WAS SUCH A JERK TODAY.
HE WAS TOTALLY IGNORING ME.
THINK HE'S MAD?

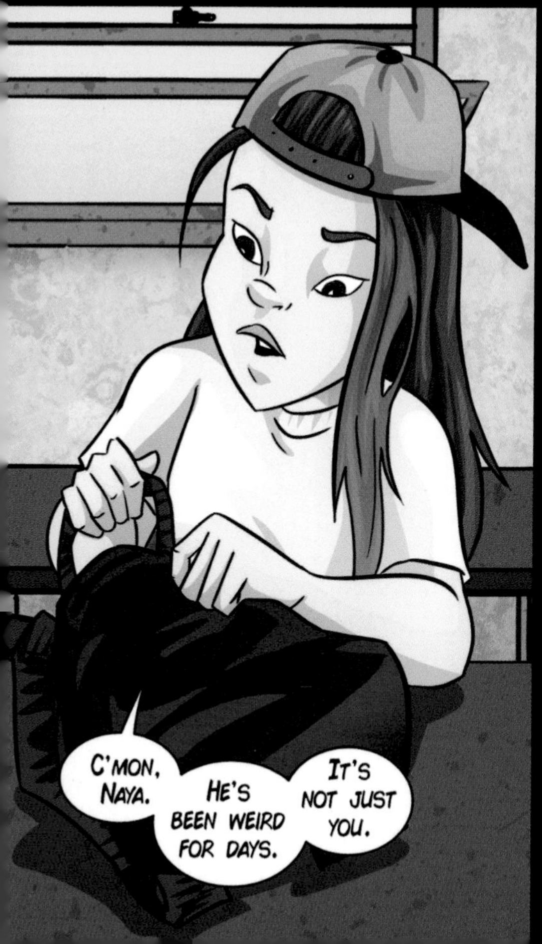
C'MON, NAYA.
HE'S BEEN WEIRD FOR DAYS.
IT'S NOT JUST YOU.

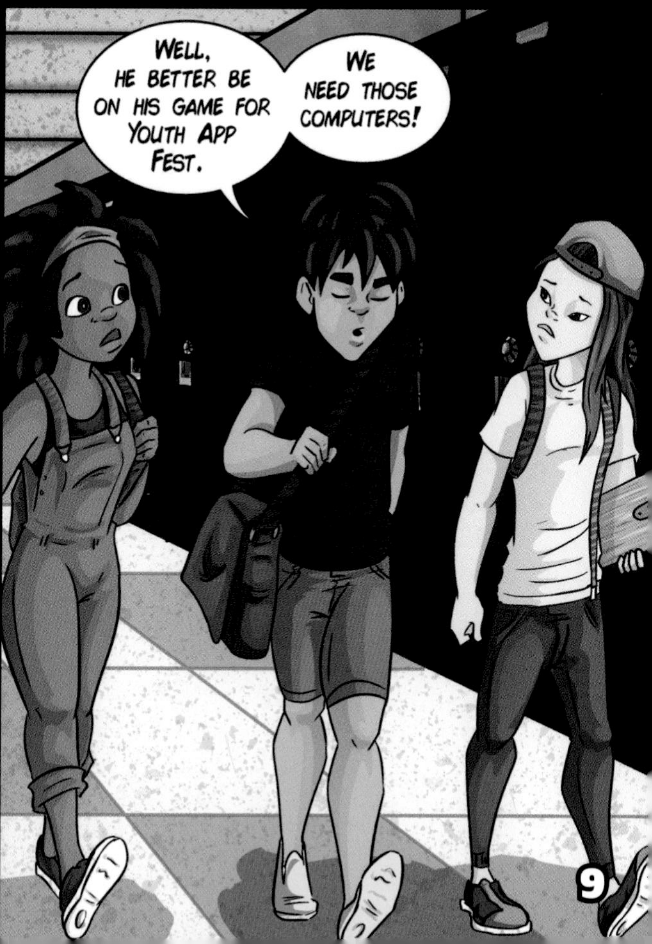
WELL, HE BETTER BE ON HIS GAME FOR YOUTH APP FEST.
WE NEED THOSE COMPUTERS!

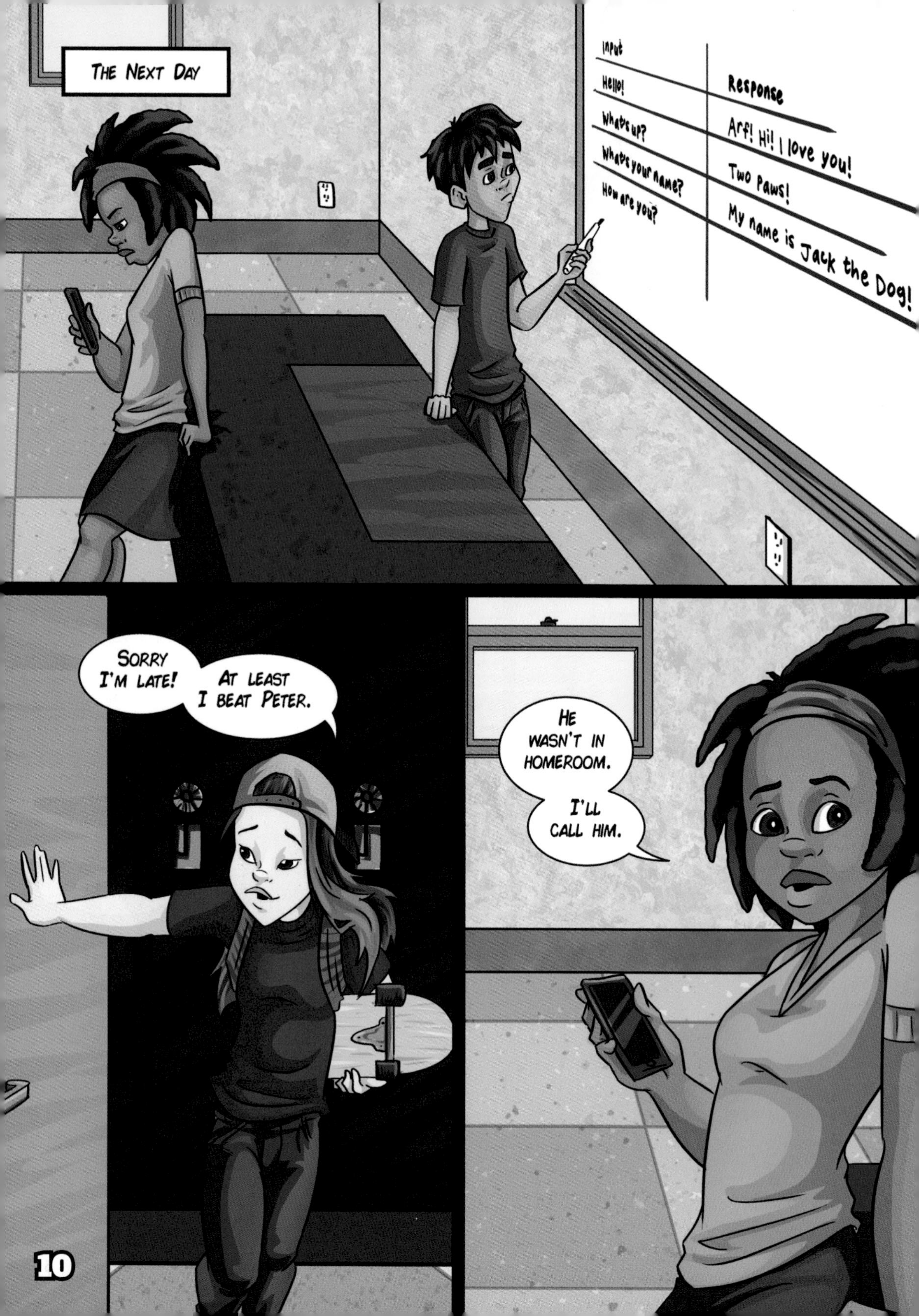
THE NEXT DAY
Input
Hello!
What's up?
What's your name?
How are you?
Response
Arf! Hi! I love you!
Two Paws!
My name is Jack the Dog!
SORRY I'M LATE!
AT LEAST I BEAT PETER.
HE WASN'T IN HOMEROOM.
I'LL CALL HIM.

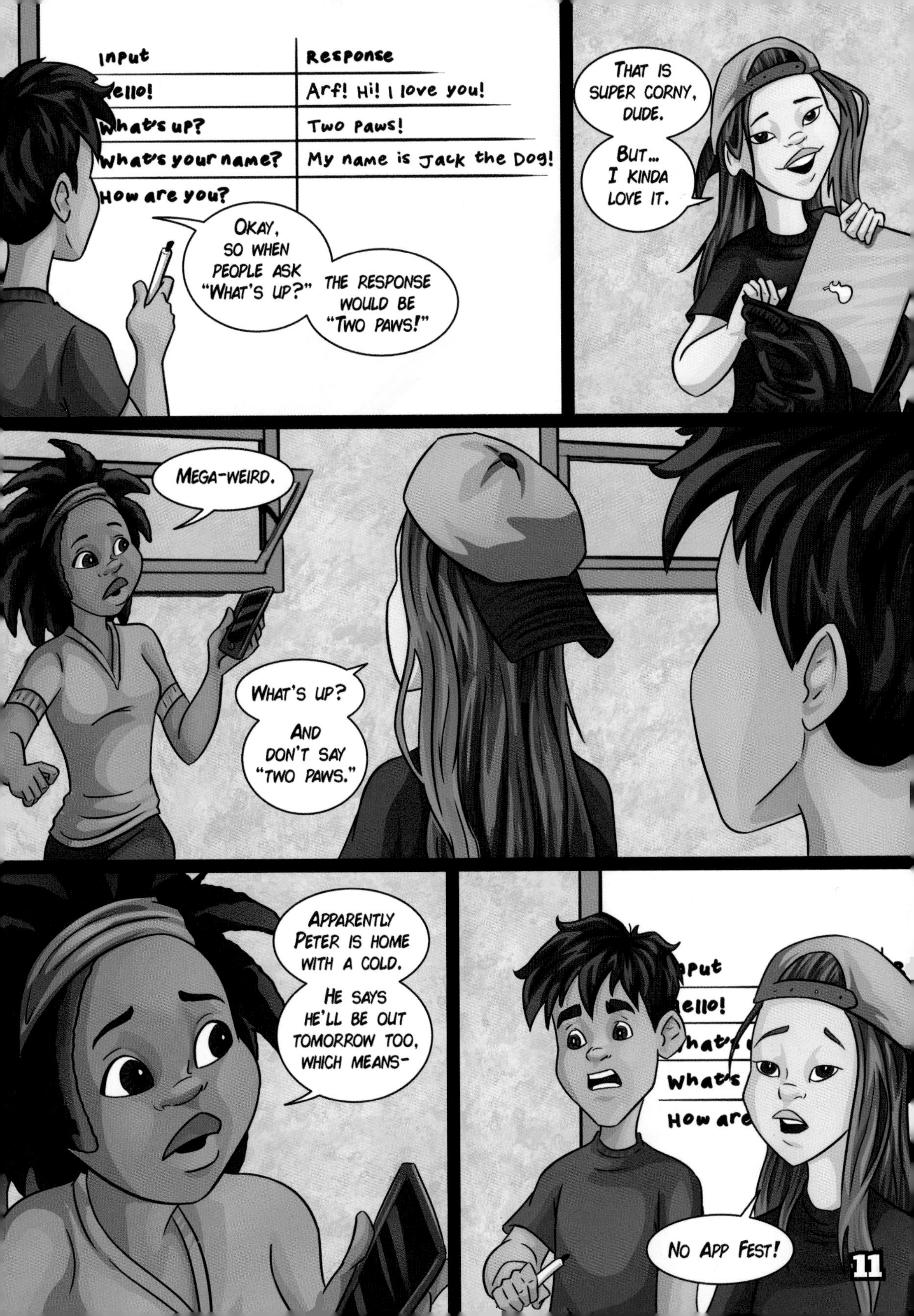

Input
Response
Hello!
Arf! Hi! I love you!
What's up?
Two Paws!
What's your name?
My name is Jack the Dog!
How are you?
OKAY, SO WHEN PEOPLE ASK "WHAT'S UP?"
THE RESPONSE WOULD BE "TWO PAWS!"
THAT IS SUPER CORNY, DUDE.
BUT... I KINDA LOVE IT.
MEGA-WEIRD.
WHAT'S UP?
AND DON'T SAY "TWO PAWS."
APPARENTLY PETER IS HOME WITH A COLD.
HE SAYS HE'LL BE OUT TOMORROW TOO, WHICH MEANS-
NO APP FEST!

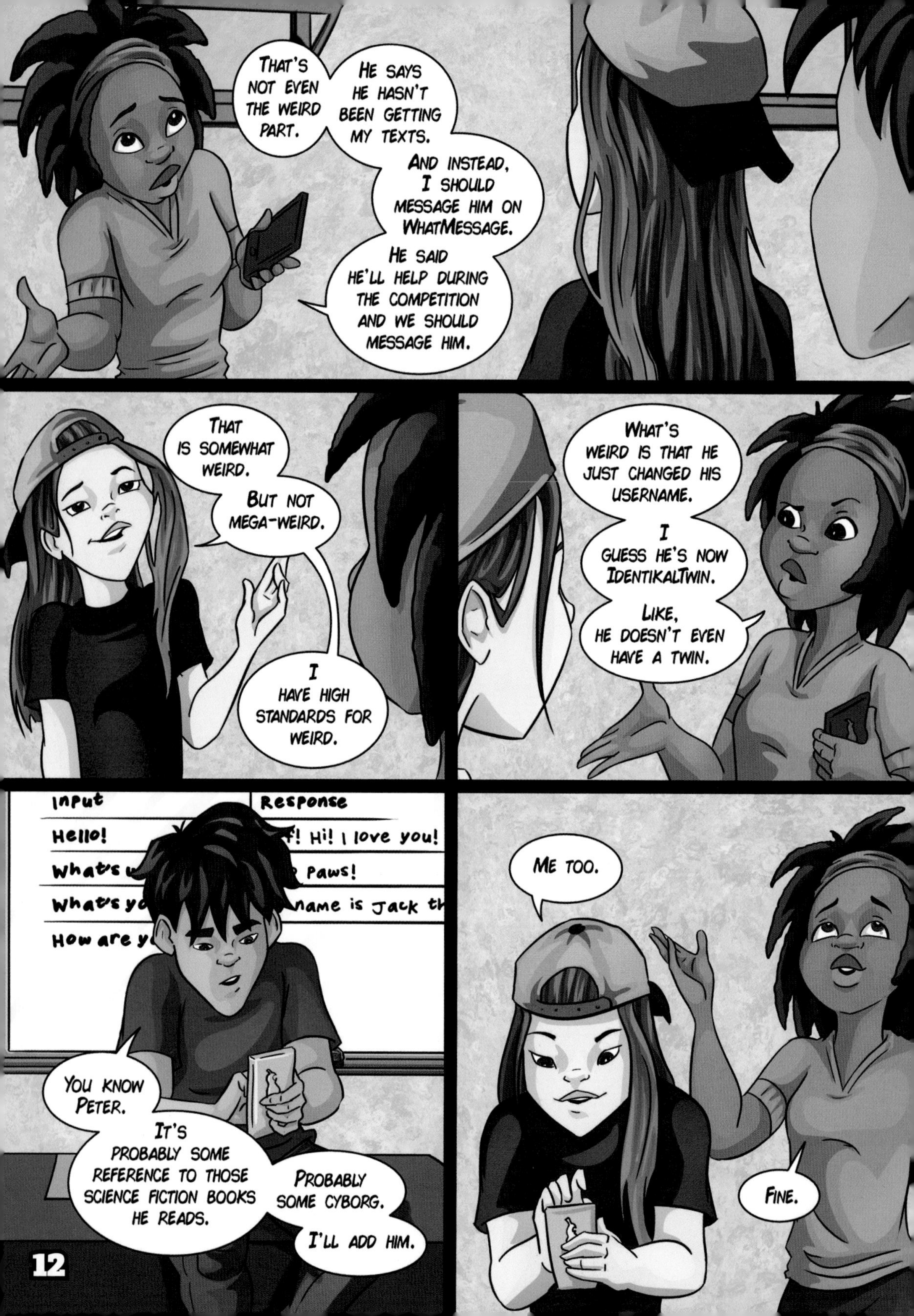

THAT'S NOT EVEN THE WEIRD PART.
HE SAYS HE HASN'T BEEN GETTING MY TEXTS.
AND INSTEAD, I SHOULD MESSAGE HIM ON WHATMESSAGE.
HE SAID HE'LL HELP DURING THE COMPETITION AND WE SHOULD MESSAGE HIM.
THAT IS SOMEWHAT WEIRD.
BUT NOT MEGA-WEIRD.
I HAVE HIGH STANDARDS FOR WEIRD.
WHAT'S WEIRD IS THAT HE JUST CHANGED HIS USERNAME.
I GUESS HE'S NOW IDENTIKALTWIN.
LIKE, HE DOESN'T EVEN HAVE A TWIN.
Input
Response
Hello!
Hi! I love you!
paws!
name is Jack
YOU KNOW PETER.
IT'S PROBABLY SOME REFERENCE TO THOSE SCIENCE FICTION BOOKS HE READS.
PROBABLY SOME CYBORG.
I'LL ADD HIM.
ME TOO.
FINE.

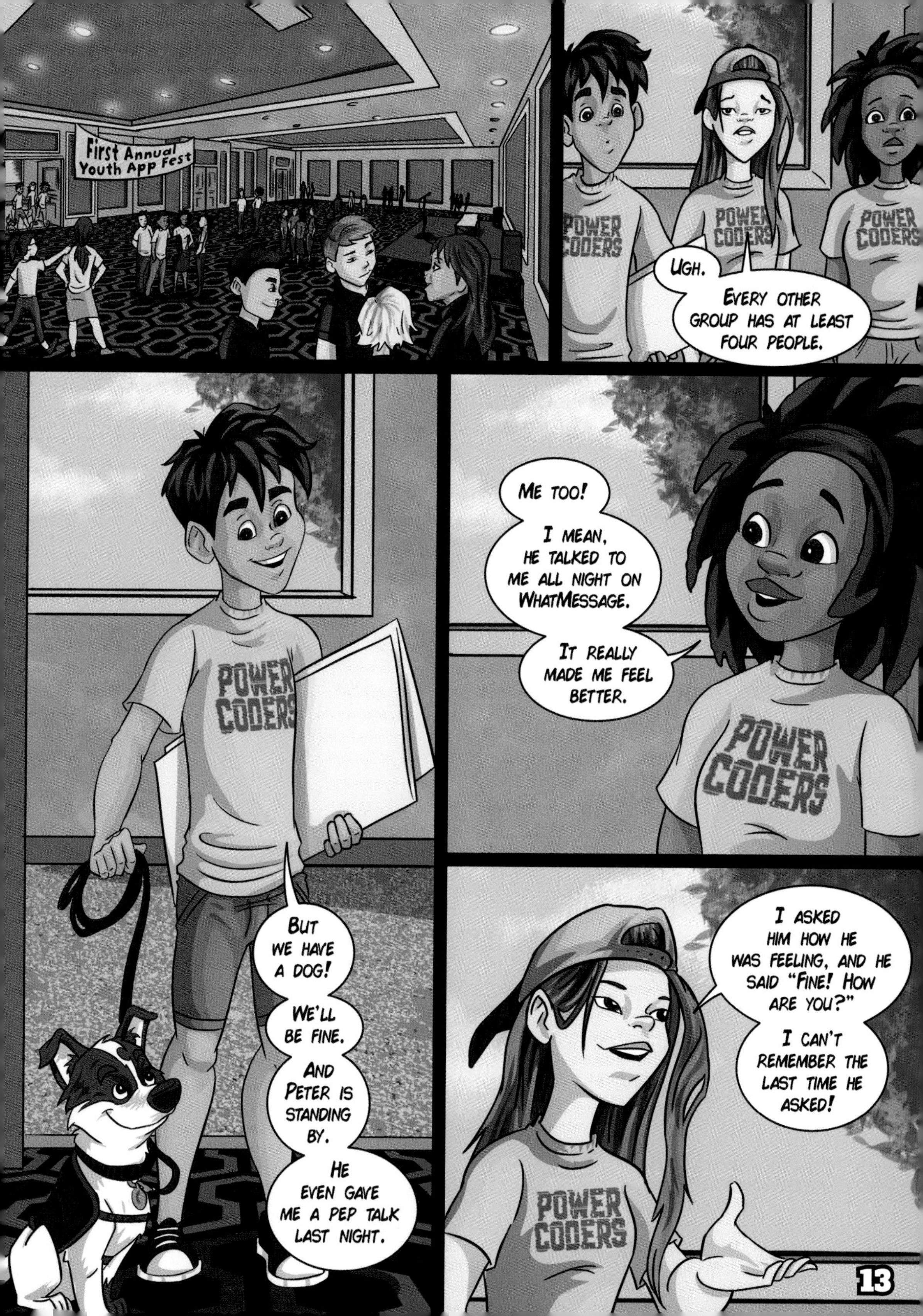
First Annual Youth App Fest
POWER CODERS
UGH.
EVERY OTHER GROUP HAS AT LEAST FOUR PEOPLE.
BUT WE HAVE A DOG!
WE'LL BE FINE.
AND PETER IS STANDING BY.
HE EVEN GAVE ME A PEP TALK LAST NIGHT.
ME TOO!
I MEAN, HE TALKED TO ME ALL NIGHT ON WHATMESSAGE.
IT REALLY MADE ME FEEL BETTER.
I ASKED HIM HOW HE WAS FEELING, AND HE SAID "FINE! HOW ARE YOU?"
I CAN'T REMEMBER THE LAST TIME HE ASKED!

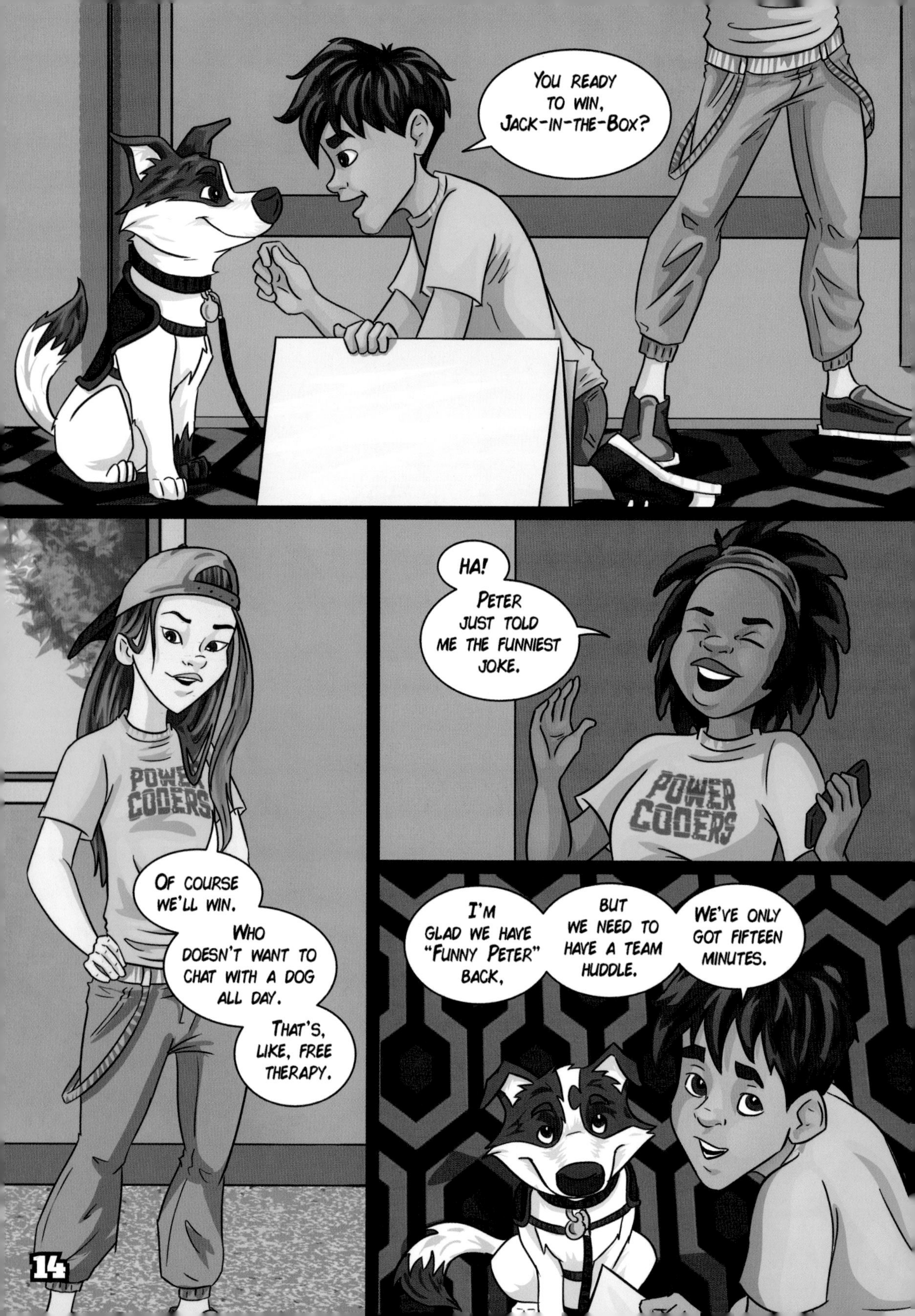
YOU READY TO WIN, JACK-IN-THE-BOX?
OF COURSE WE'LL WIN.
WHO DOESN'T WANT TO CHAT WITH A DOG ALL DAY.
THAT'S, LIKE, FREE THERAPY.
POWER CODERS
HA!
PETER JUST TOLD ME THE FUNNIEST JOKE.
POWER CODERS
I'M GLAD WE HAVE "FUNNY PETER" BACK,
BUT WE NEED TO HAVE A TEAM HUDDLE.
WE'VE ONLY GOT FIFTEEN MINUTES.

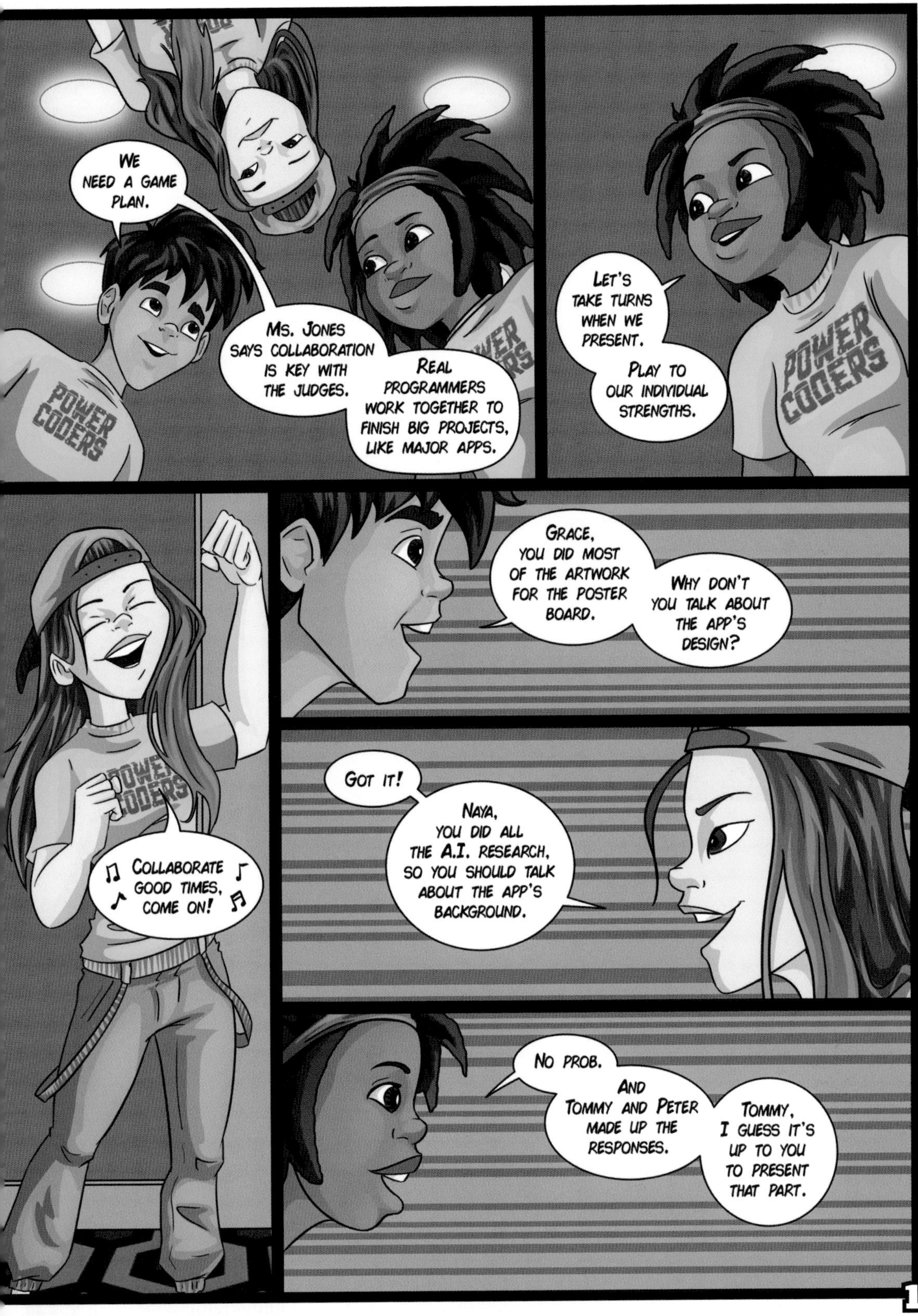

WE NEED A GAME PLAN.
MS. JONES SAYS COLLABORATION IS KEY WITH THE JUDGES.
REAL PROGRAMMERS WORK TOGETHER TO FINISH BIG PROJECTS, LIKE MAJOR APPS.
LET'S TAKE TURNS WHEN WE PRESENT.
PLAY TO OUR INDIVIDUAL STRENGTHS.
GRACE, YOU DID MOST OF THE ARTWORK FOR THE POSTER BOARD.
WHY DON'T YOU TALK ABOUT THE APP'S DESIGN?
♫ COLLABORATE GOOD TIMES, COME ON! ♫
GOT IT!
NAYA, YOU DID ALL THE A.I. RESEARCH, SO YOU SHOULD TALK ABOUT THE APP'S BACKGROUND.
NO PROB.
AND TOMMY AND PETER MADE UP THE RESPONSES.
TOMMY, I GUESS IT'S UP TO YOU TO PRESENT THAT PART.

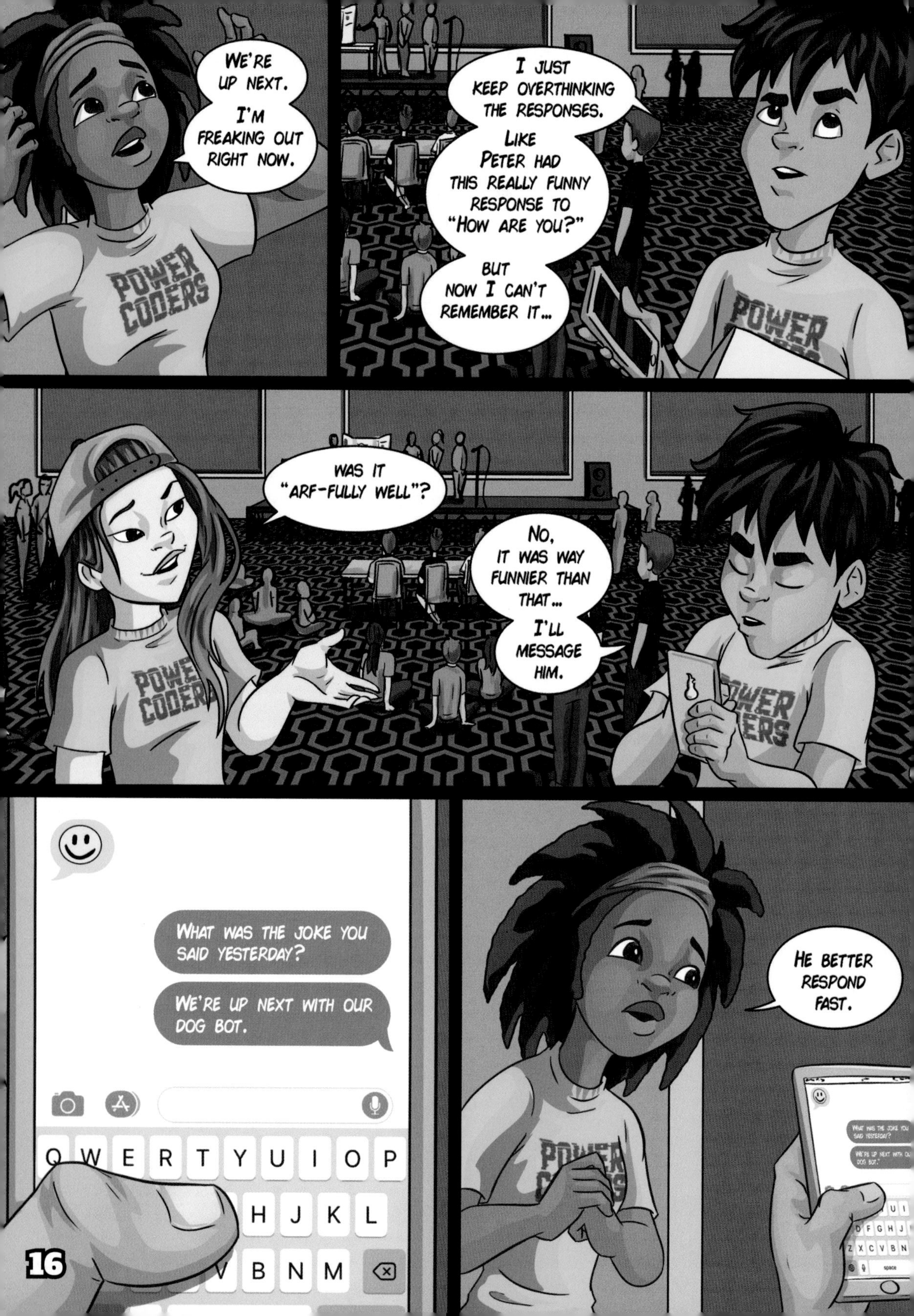
WE'RE UP NEXT.
I'M FREAKING OUT RIGHT NOW.
I JUST KEEP OVERTHINKING THE RESPONSES.
LIKE PETER HAD THIS REALLY FUNNY RESPONSE TO "HOW ARE YOU?"
BUT NOW I CAN'T REMEMBER IT...
WAS IT "ARF-FULLY WELL"?
NO, IT WAS WAY FUNNIER THAN THAT...
I'LL MESSAGE HIM.
WHAT WAS THE JOKE YOU SAID YESTERDAY?
WE'RE UP NEXT WITH OUR DOG BOT.
Q W E R T Y U I O P
H J K L
V B N M
HE BETTER RESPOND FAST.

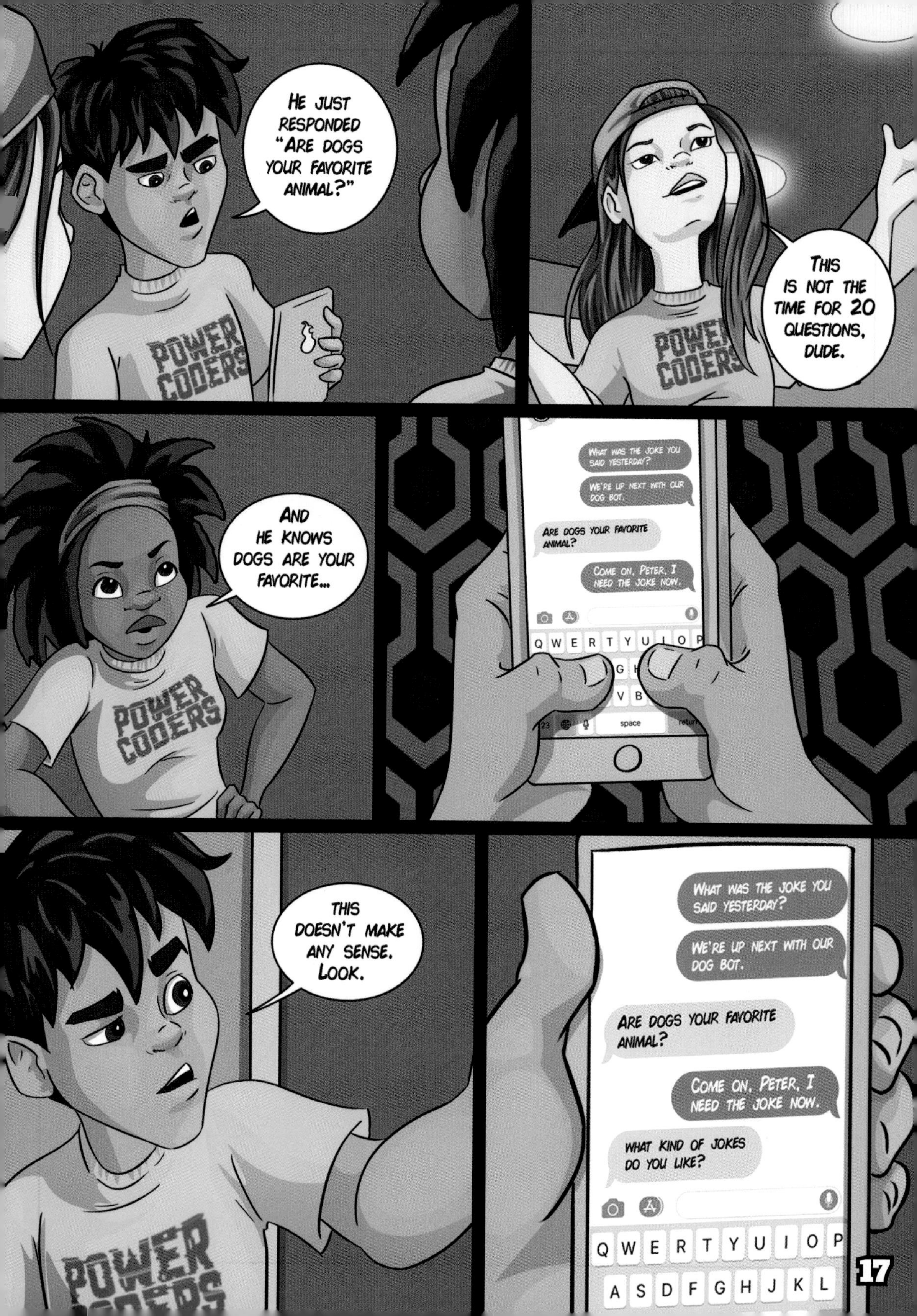

HE JUST RESPONDED "ARE DOGS YOUR FAVORITE ANIMAL?"
THIS IS NOT THE TIME FOR 20 QUESTIONS, DUDE.
AND HE KNOWS DOGS ARE YOUR FAVORITE...
WHAT WAS THE JOKE YOU SAID YESTERDAY?
WE'RE UP NEXT WITH OUR DOG BOT.
ARE DOGS YOUR FAVORITE ANIMAL?
COME ON, PETER. I NEED THE JOKE NOW.
THIS DOESN'T MAKE ANY SENSE. LOOK.
WHAT WAS THE JOKE YOU SAID YESTERDAY?
WE'RE UP NEXT WITH OUR DOG BOT.
ARE DOGS YOUR FAVORITE ANIMAL?
COME ON, PETER. I NEED THE JOKE NOW.
WHAT KIND OF JOKES DO YOU LIKE?

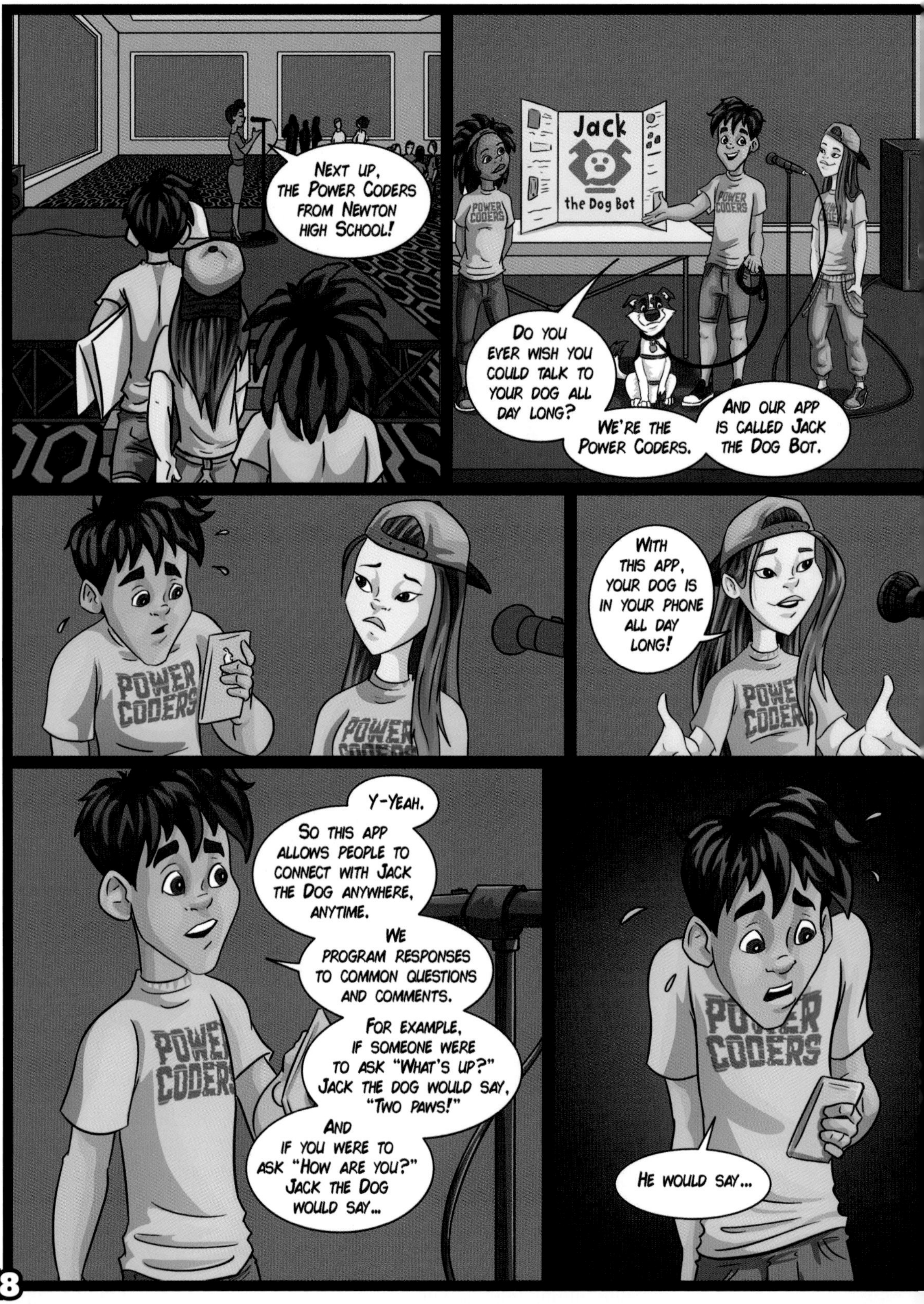

Next up, the Power Coders from Newton high School!
Jack
the Dog Bot
Do you ever wish you could talk to your dog all day long?
We're the Power Coders.
And our app is called Jack the Dog Bot.
With this app, your dog is in your phone all day long!
Y-Yeah.
So this app allows people to connect with Jack the Dog anywhere, anytime.
We program responses to common questions and comments.
For example, if someone were to ask "What's up?" Jack the dog would say, "Two paws!"
And if you were to ask "How are you?" Jack the Dog would say...
He would say...

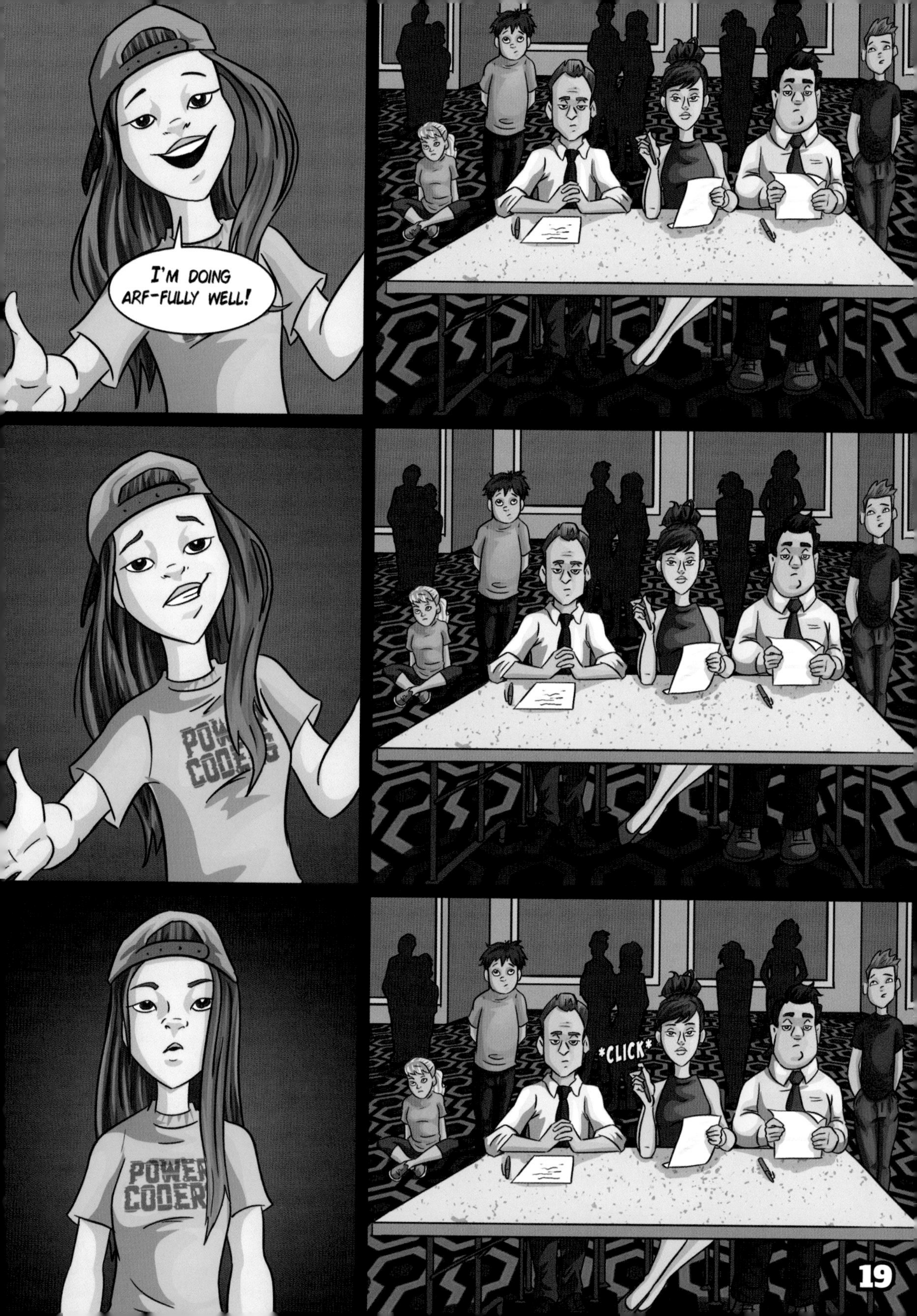
I'M DOING ARF-FULLY WELL!
POWER CODERS
POWER CODERS
CLICK

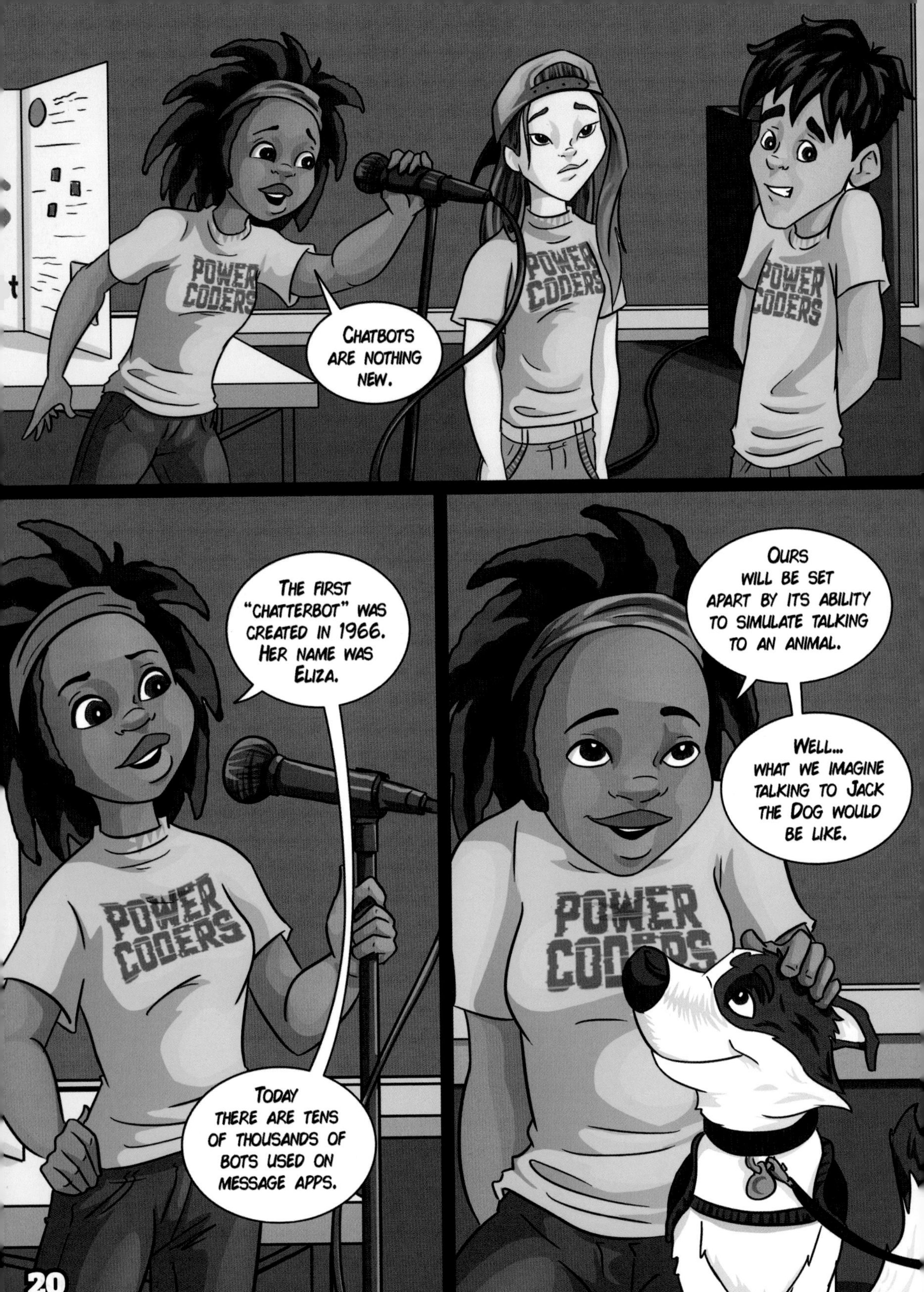
CHATBOTS ARE NOTHING NEW.
THE FIRST "CHATTERBOT" WAS CREATED IN 1966. HER NAME WAS ELIZA.
TODAY THERE ARE TENS OF THOUSANDS OF BOTS USED ON MESSAGE APPS.
OURS WILL BE SET APART BY ITS ABILITY TO SIMULATE TALKING TO AN ANIMAL.
WELL... WHAT WE IMAGINE TALKING TO JACK THE DOG WOULD BE LIKE.
POWER CODERS

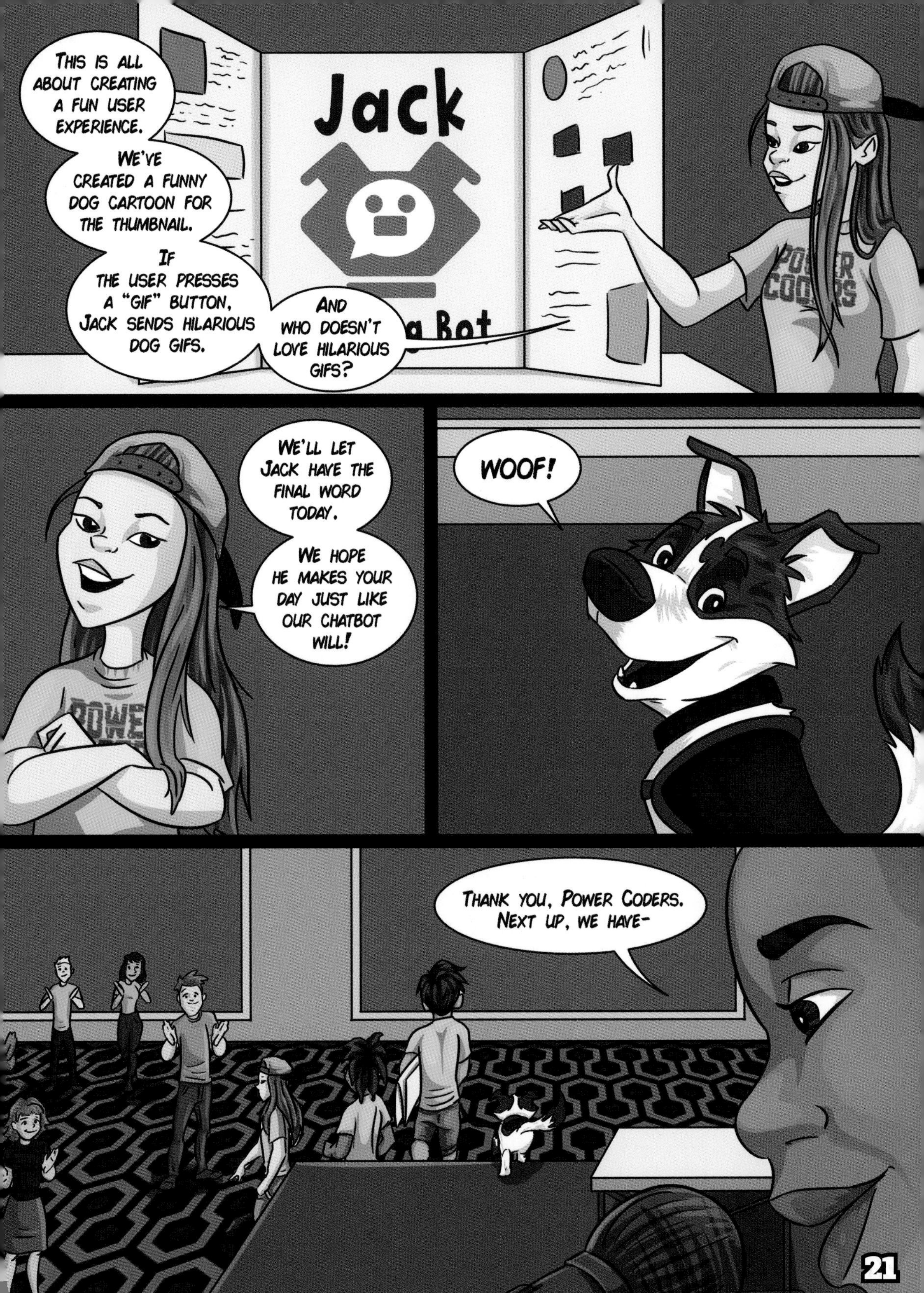
THIS IS ALL ABOUT CREATING A FUN USER EXPERIENCE.
WE'VE CREATED A FUNNY DOG CARTOON FOR THE THUMBNAIL.
IF THE USER PRESSES A "GIF" BUTTON, JACK SENDS HILARIOUS DOG GIFS.
AND WHO DOESN'T LOVE HILARIOUS GIFS?
Jack
WE'LL LET JACK HAVE THE FINAL WORD TODAY.
WE HOPE HE MAKES YOUR DAY JUST LIKE OUR CHATBOT WILL!
WOOF!
THANK YOU, POWER CODERS. NEXT UP, WE HAVE-

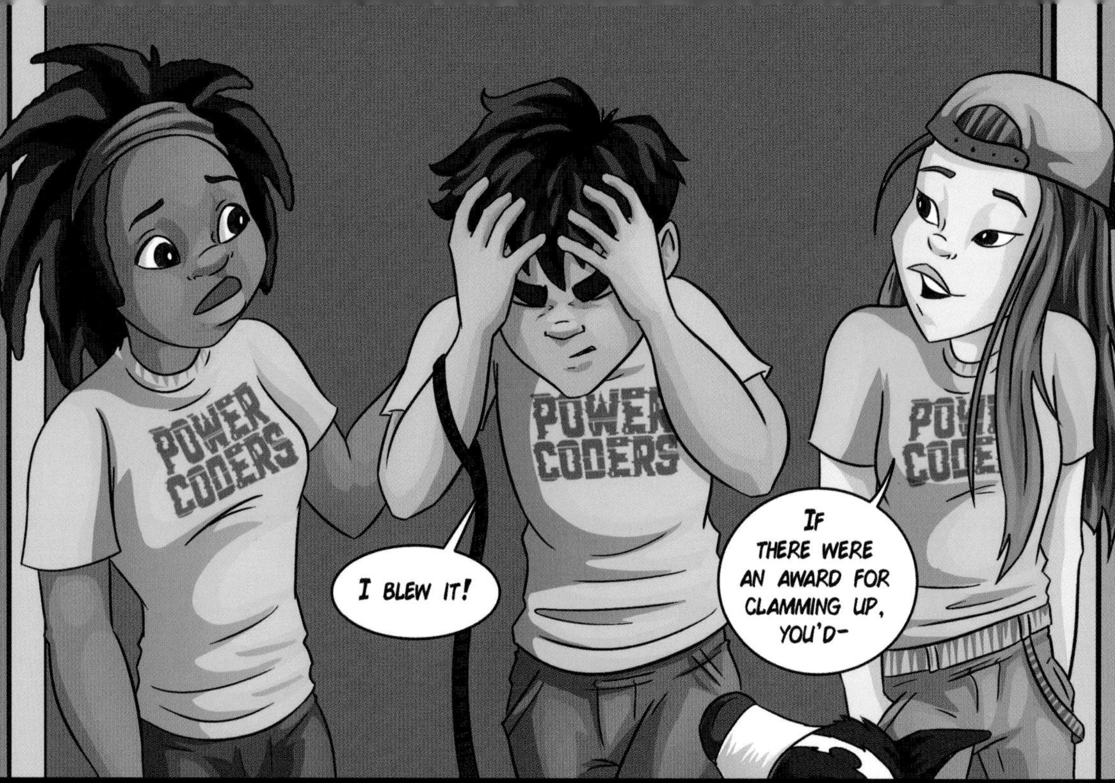
POWER CODERS
I BLEW IT!
IF THERE WERE AN AWARD FOR CLAMMING UP, YOU'D-

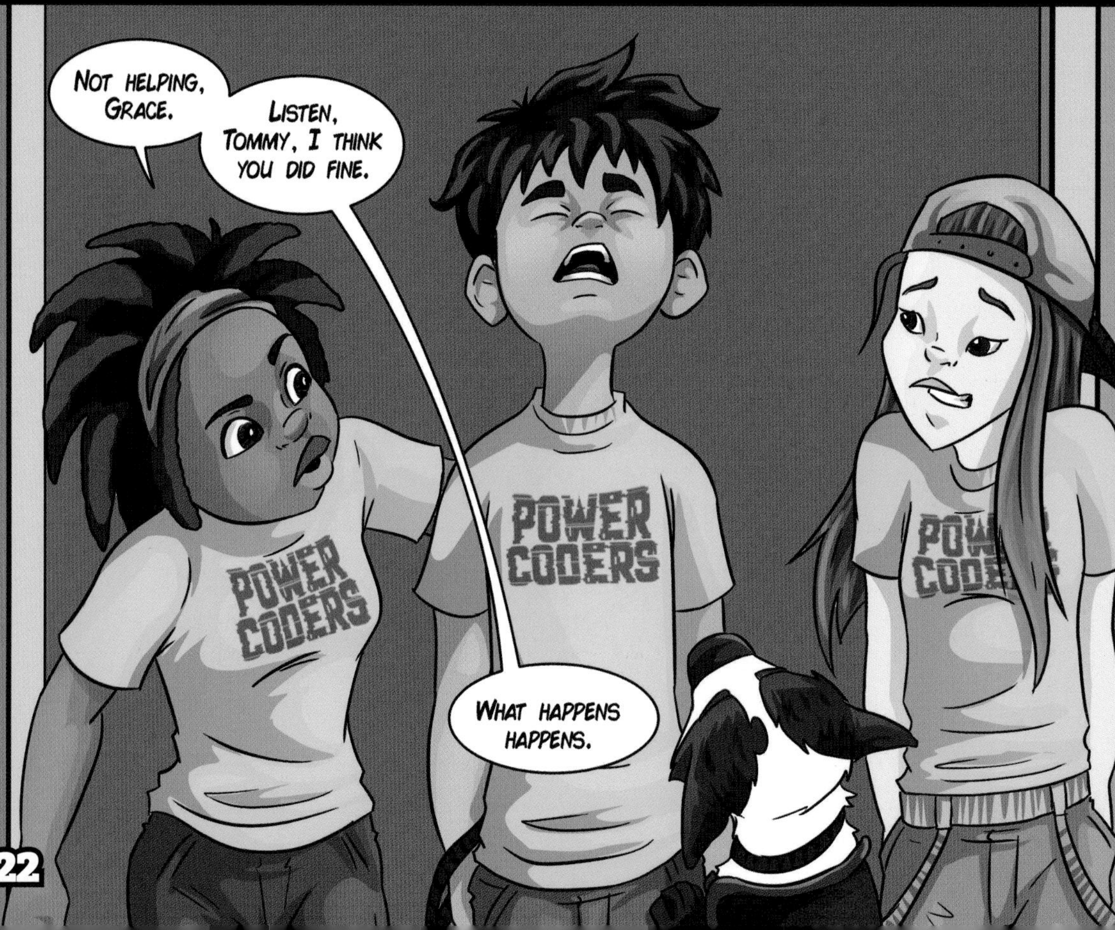
NOT HELPING, GRACE.
LISTEN, TOMMY, I THINK YOU DID FINE.
WHAT HAPPENS HAPPENS.
POWER CODERS

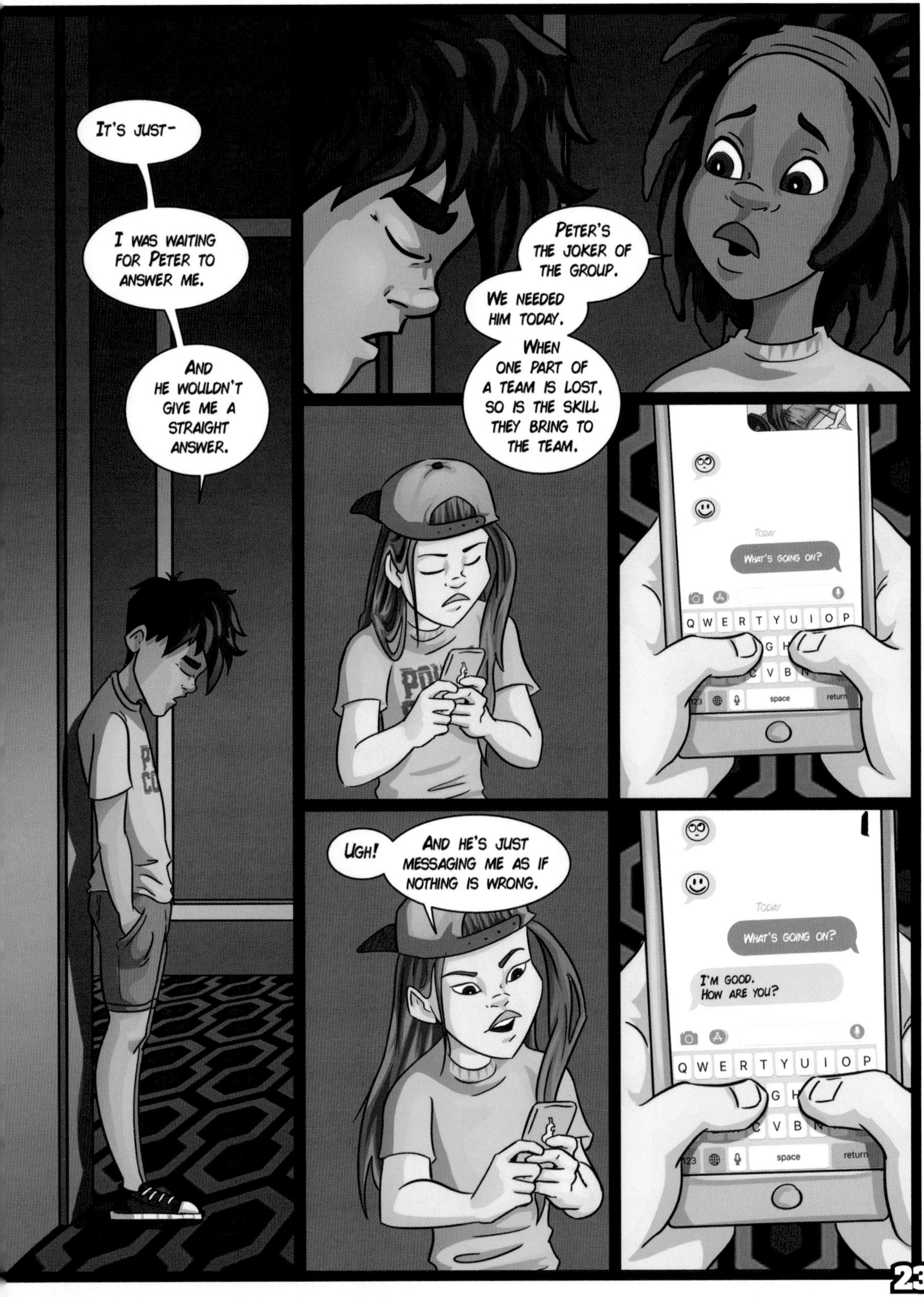

It's just-
I was waiting for Peter to answer me.
And he wouldn't give me a straight answer.
Peter's the joker of the group.
We needed him today.
When one part of a team is lost, so is the skill they bring to the team.
Today
What's going on?
Ugh!
And he's just messaging me as if nothing is wrong.
Today
What's going on?
I'm good. How are you?

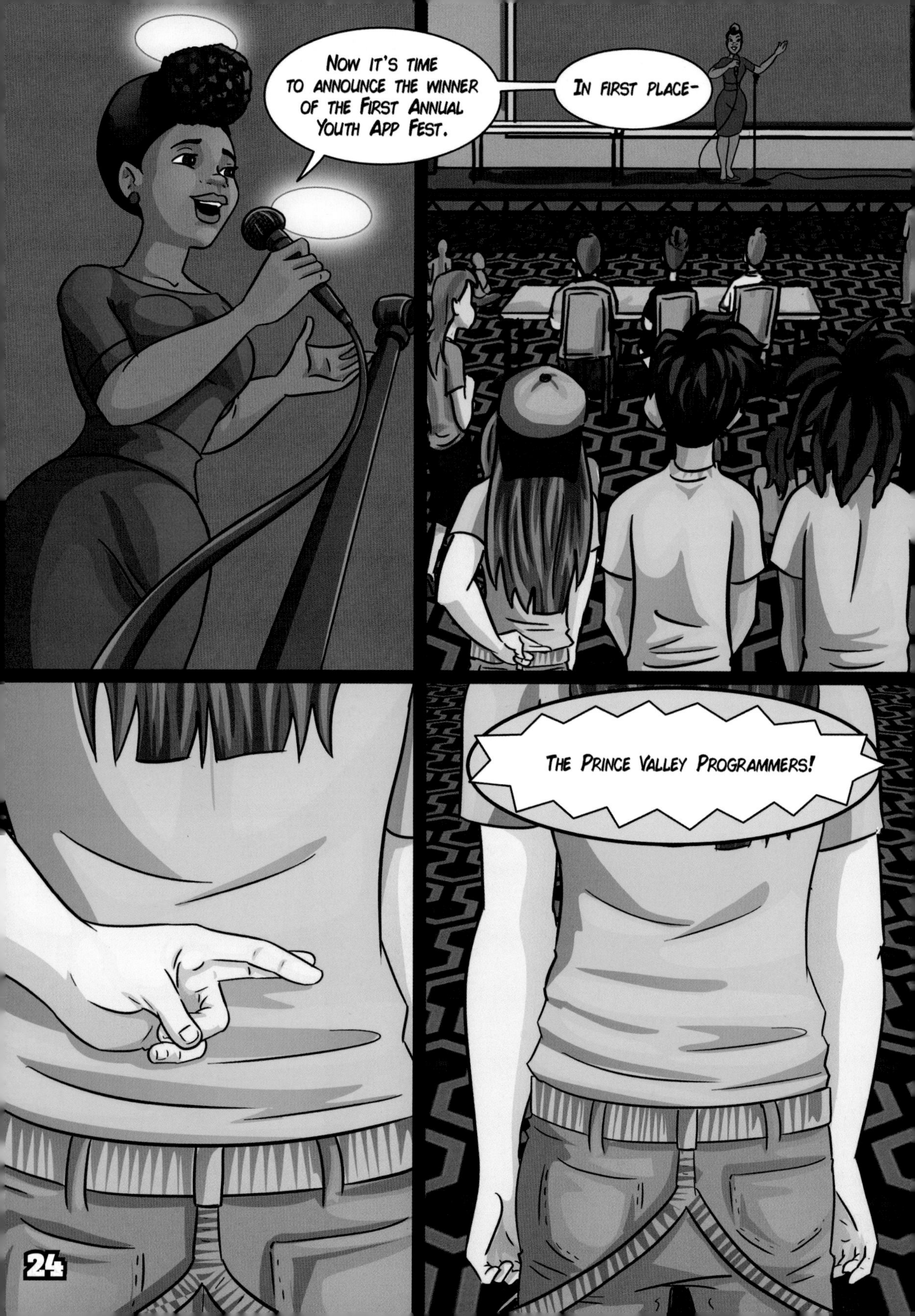
NOW IT'S TIME TO ANNOUNCE THE WINNER OF THE FIRST ANNUAL YOUTH APP FEST.
IN FIRST PLACE-
THE PRINCE VALLEY PROGRAMMERS!

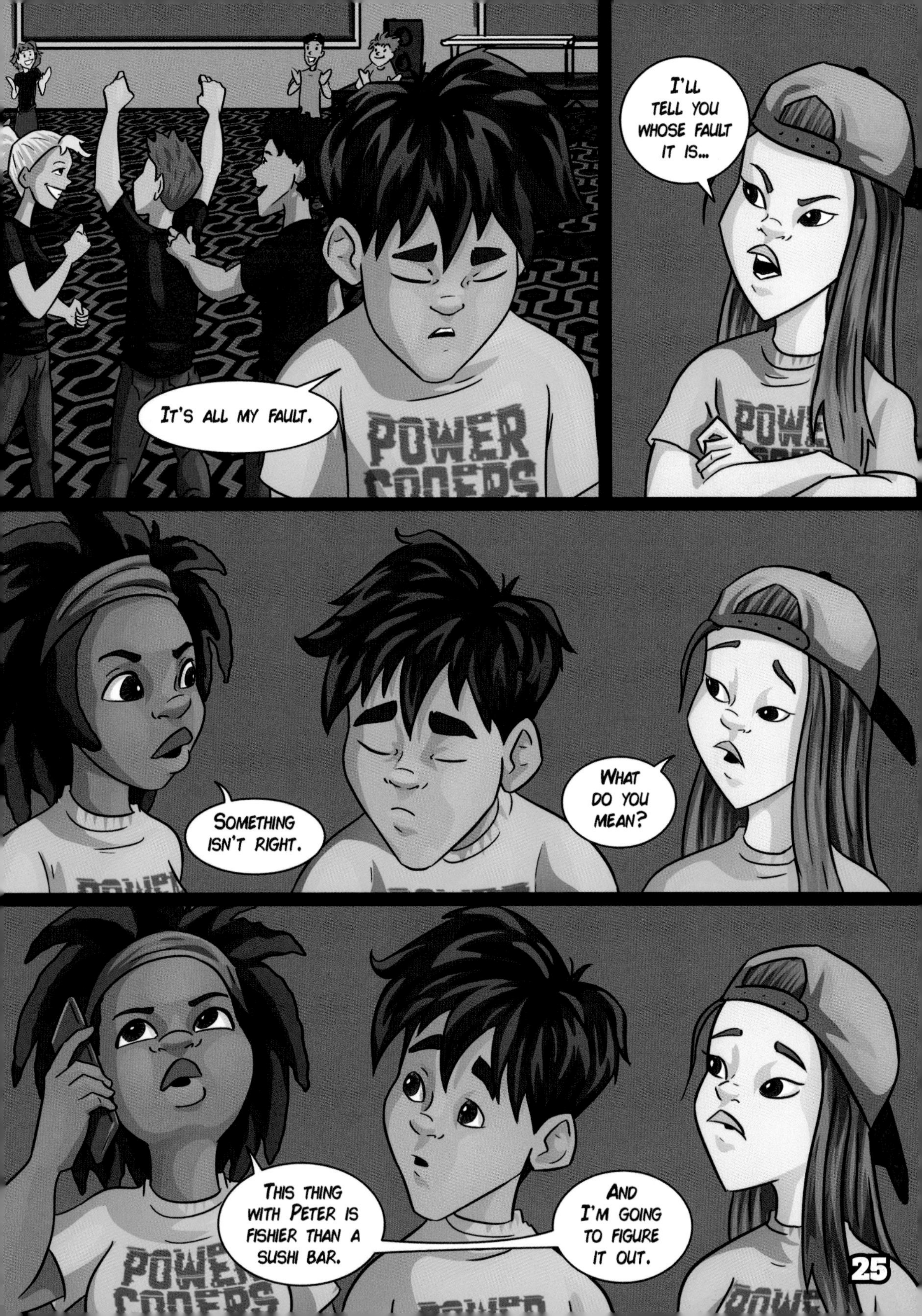
IT'S ALL MY FAULT.
I'LL TELL YOU WHOSE FAULT IT IS...
SOMETHING ISN'T RIGHT.
WHAT DO YOU MEAN?
THIS THING WITH PETER IS FISHIER THAN A SUSHI BAR.
AND I'M GOING TO FIGURE IT OUT.

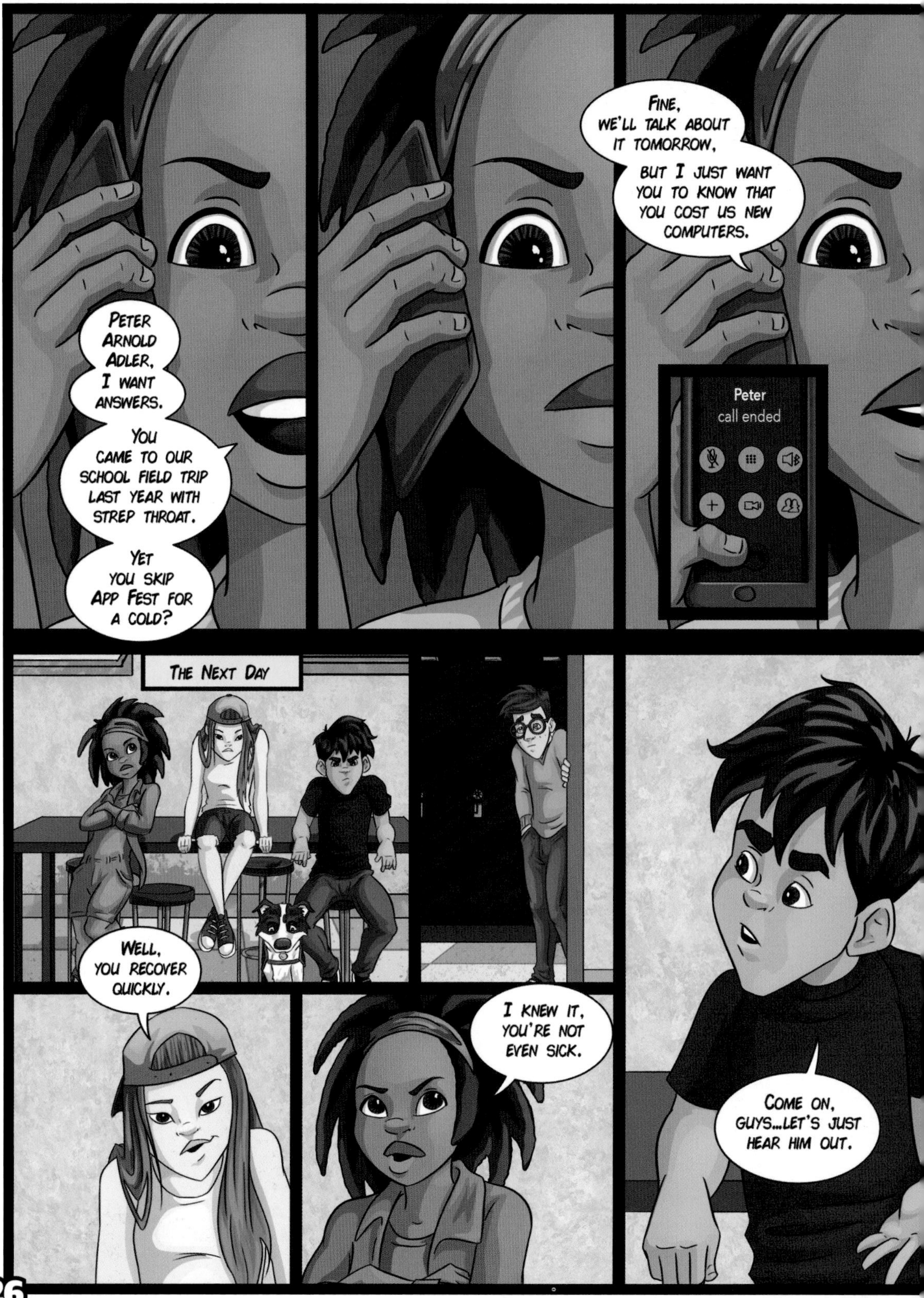
Peter Arnold Adler. I want answers.
You came to our school field trip last year with strep throat.
Yet you skip App Fest for a cold?
Fine, we'll talk about it tomorrow,
but I just want you to know that you cost us new computers.
Peter
call ended
The Next Day
Well, you recover quickly.
I knew it, you're not even sick.
Come on, guys...let's just hear him out.

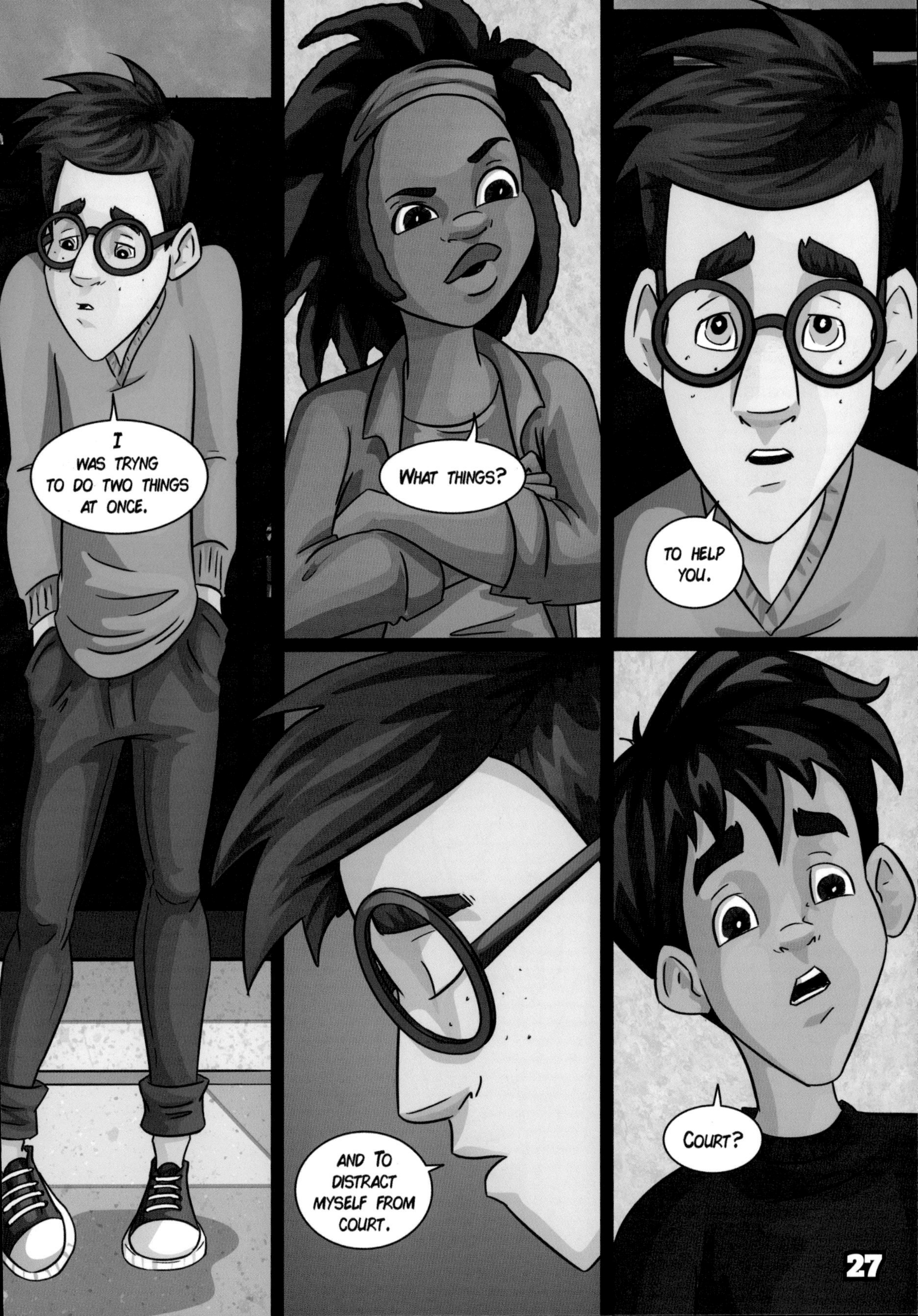
I WAS TRYNG TO DO TWO THINGS AT ONCE.
WHAT THINGS?
TO HELP YOU.
AND TO DISTRACT MYSELF FROM COURT.
COURT?

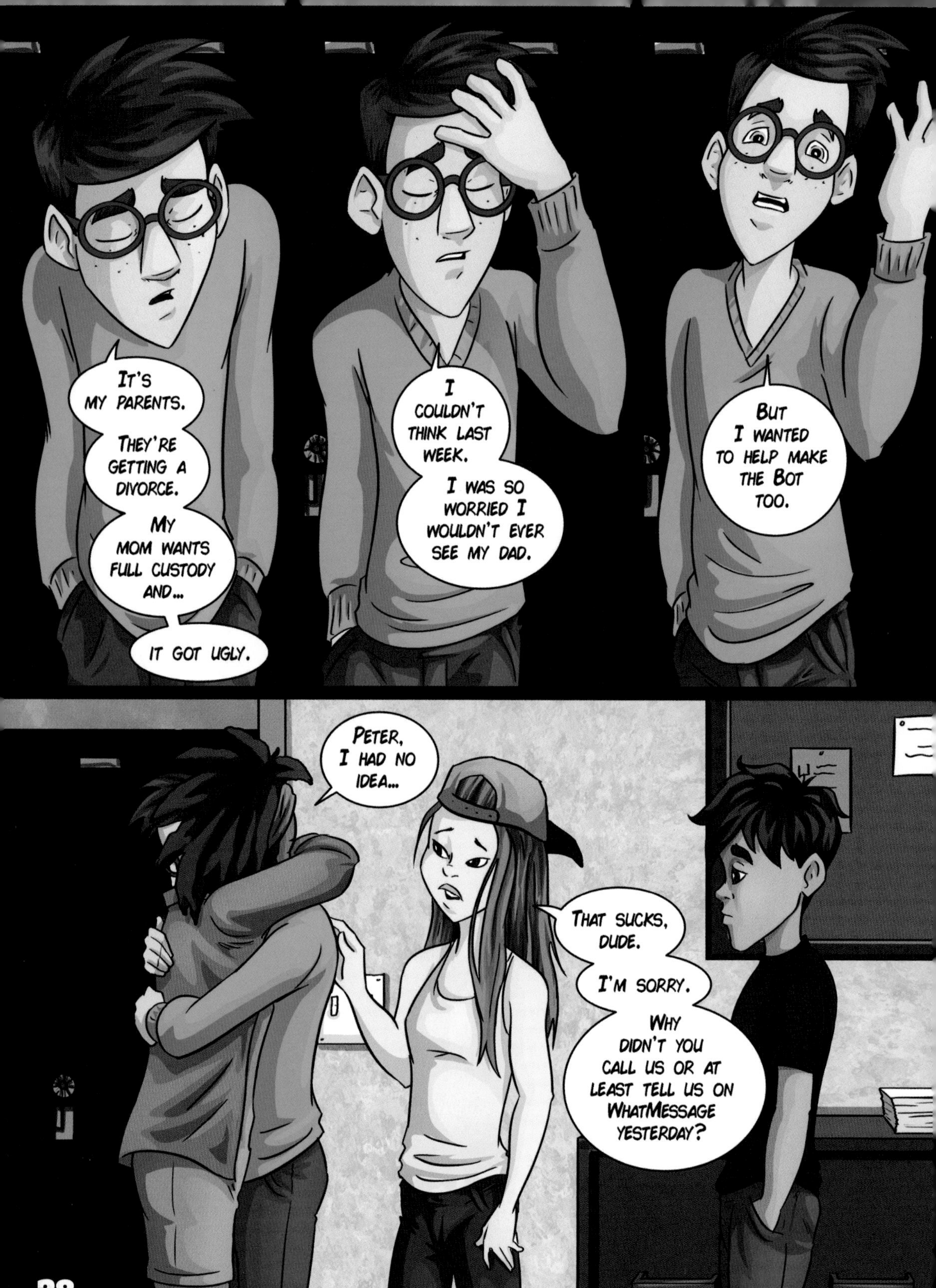
IT'S MY PARENTS.
THEY'RE GETTING A DIVORCE.
MY MOM WANTS FULL CUSTODY AND...
IT GOT UGLY.
I COULDN'T THINK LAST WEEK.
I WAS SO WORRIED I WOULDN'T EVER SEE MY DAD.
BUT I WANTED TO HELP MAKE THE BOT TOO.
PETER, I HAD NO IDEA...
THAT SUCKS, DUDE.
I'M SORRY.
WHY DIDN'T YOU CALL US OR AT LEAST TELL US ON WHATMESSAGE YESTERDAY?

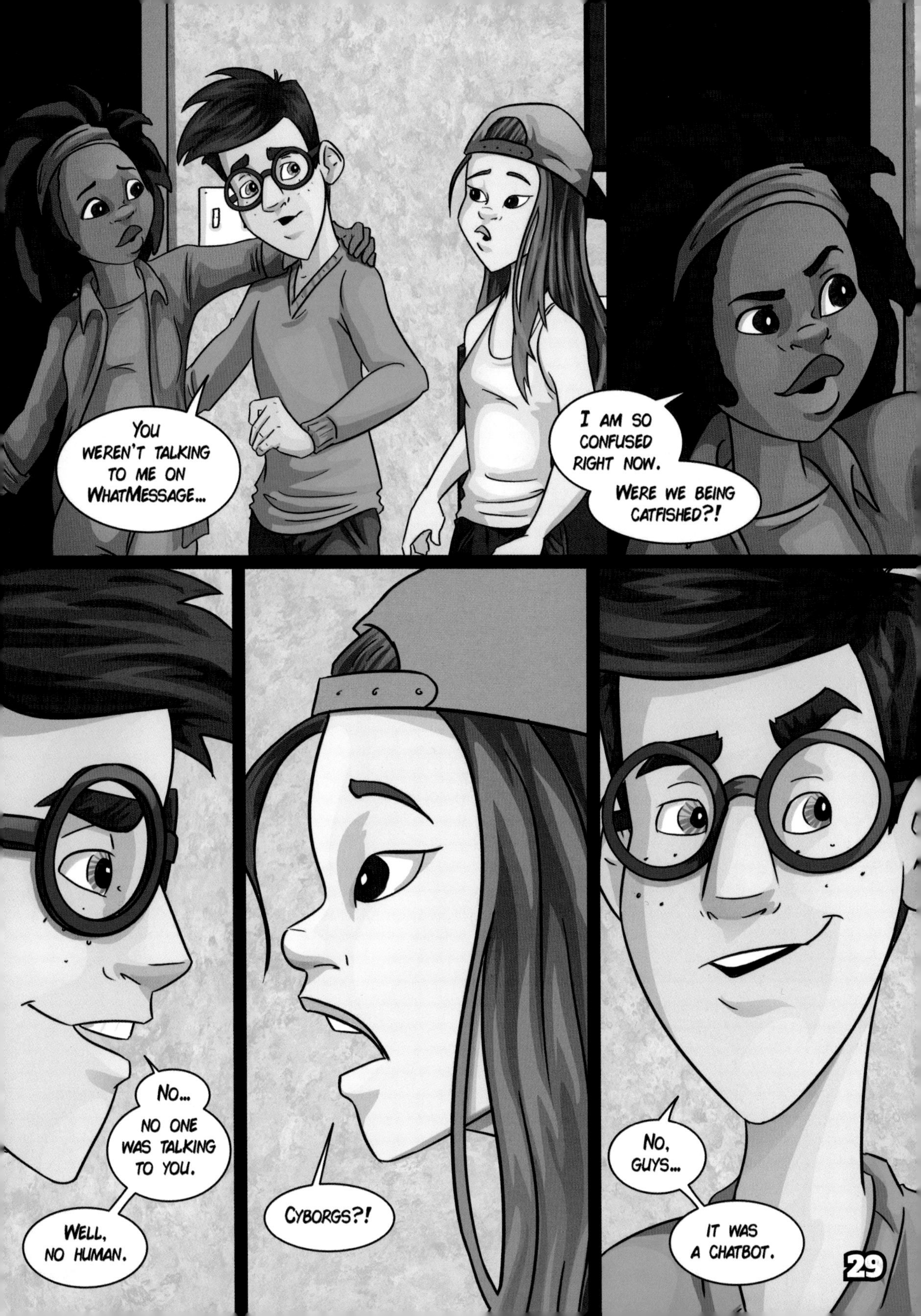
YOU WEREN'T TALKING TO ME ON WHATMESSAGE...
I AM SO CONFUSED RIGHT NOW.
WERE WE BEING CATFISHED?!
NO...
NO ONE WAS TALKING TO YOU.
WELL, NO HUMAN.
CYBORGS?!
NO, GUYS...
IT WAS A CHATBOT.

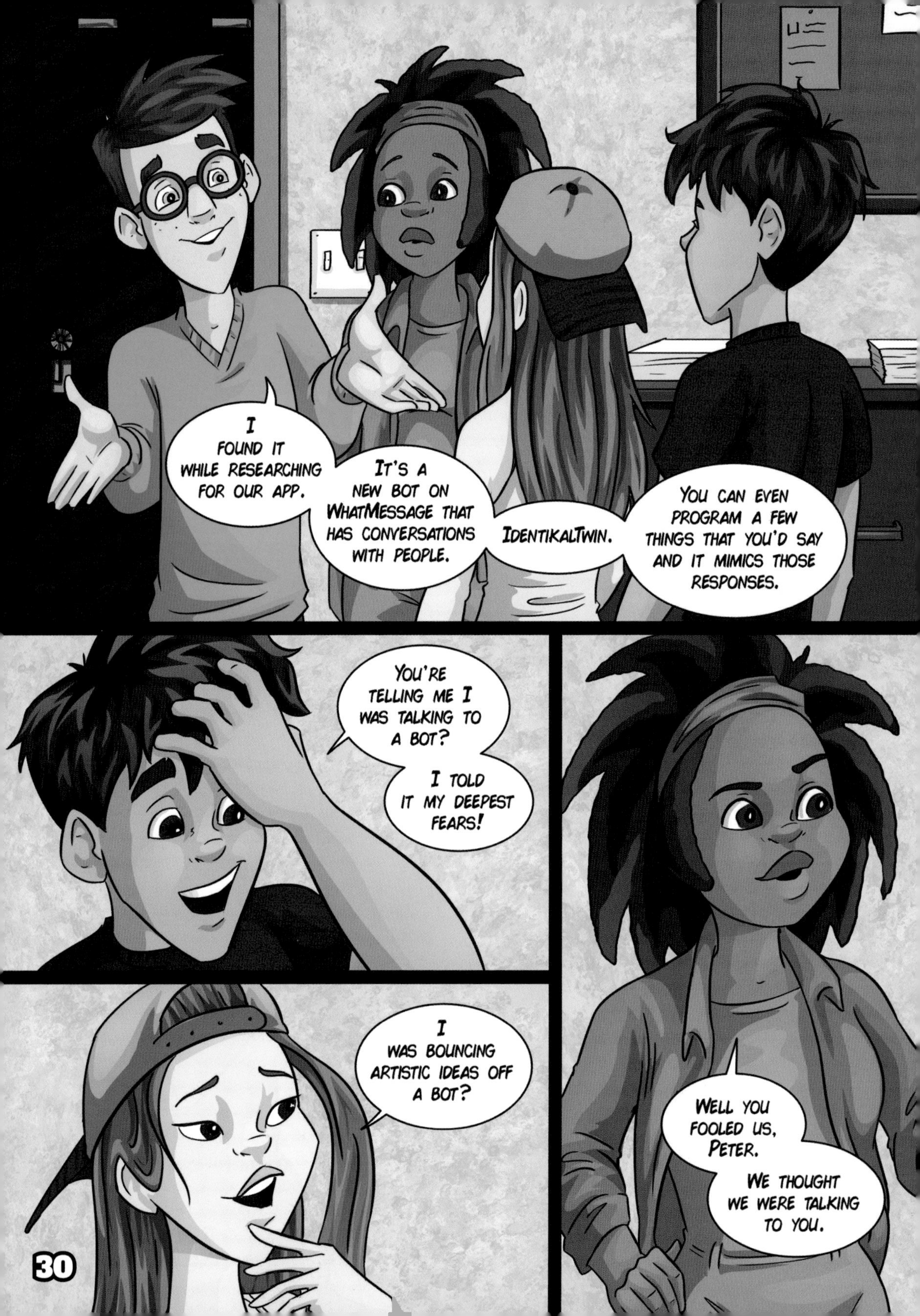

I FOUND IT WHILE RESEARCHING FOR OUR APP.
IT'S A NEW BOT ON WHATMESSAGE THAT HAS CONVERSATIONS WITH PEOPLE.
IDENTIKALTWIN.
YOU CAN EVEN PROGRAM A FEW THINGS THAT YOU'D SAY AND IT MIMICS THOSE RESPONSES.
YOU'RE TELLING ME I WAS TALKING TO A BOT?
I TOLD IT MY DEEPEST FEARS!
I WAS BOUNCING ARTISTIC IDEAS OFF A BOT?
WELL YOU FOOLED US, PETER.
WE THOUGHT WE WERE TALKING TO YOU.

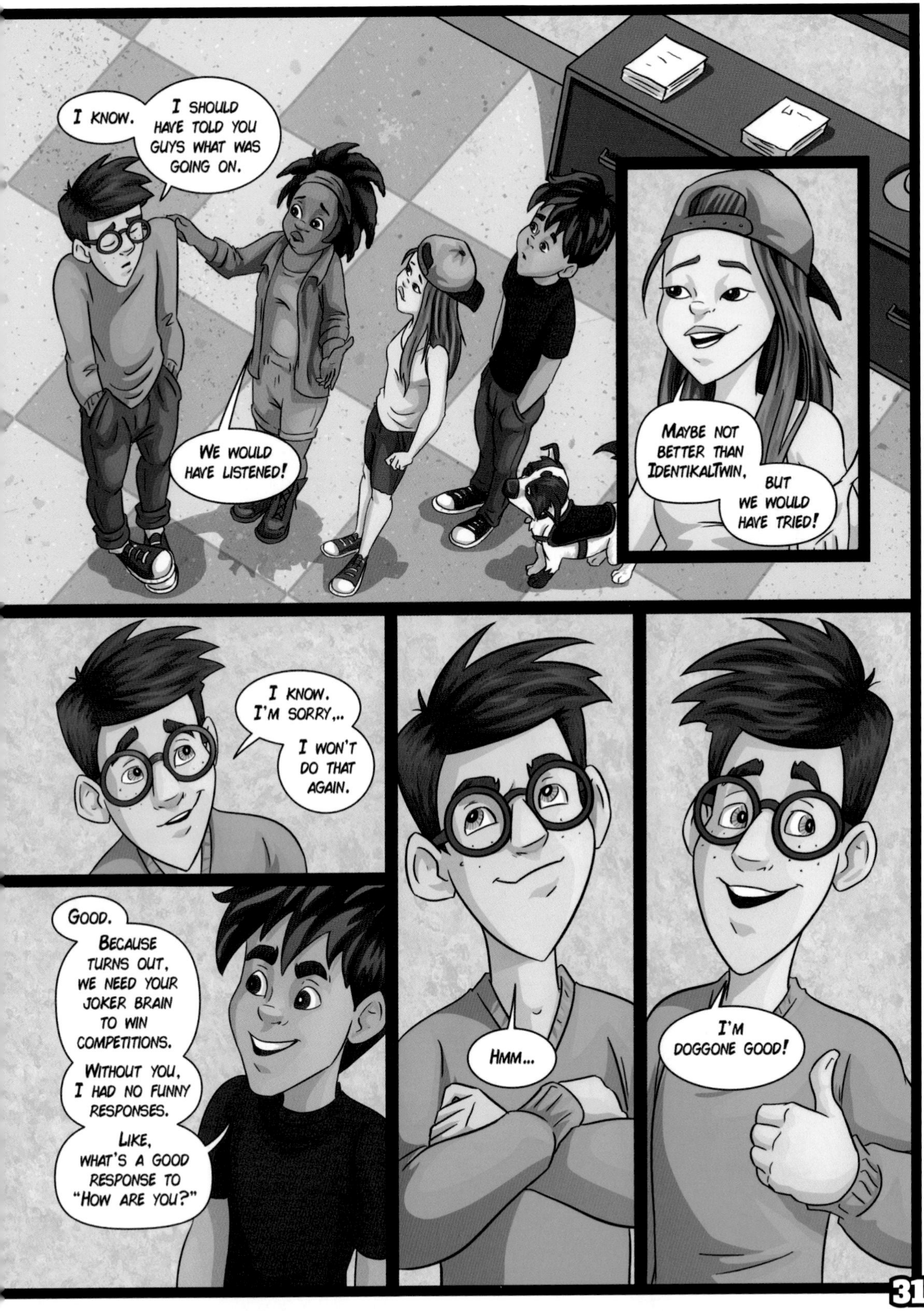
I KNOW.
I SHOULD HAVE TOLD YOU GUYS WHAT WAS GOING ON.
WE WOULD HAVE LISTENED!
MAYBE NOT BETTER THAN IDENTIKALTWIN,
BUT WE WOULD HAVE TRIED!
I KNOW. I'M SORRY...
I WON'T DO THAT AGAIN.
GOOD.
BECAUSE TURNS OUT, WE NEED YOUR JOKER BRAIN TO WIN COMPETITIONS.
WITHOUT YOU, I HAD NO FUNNY RESPONSES.
LIKE, WHAT'S A GOOD RESPONSE TO "HOW ARE YOU?"
HMM...
I'M DOGGONE GOOD!

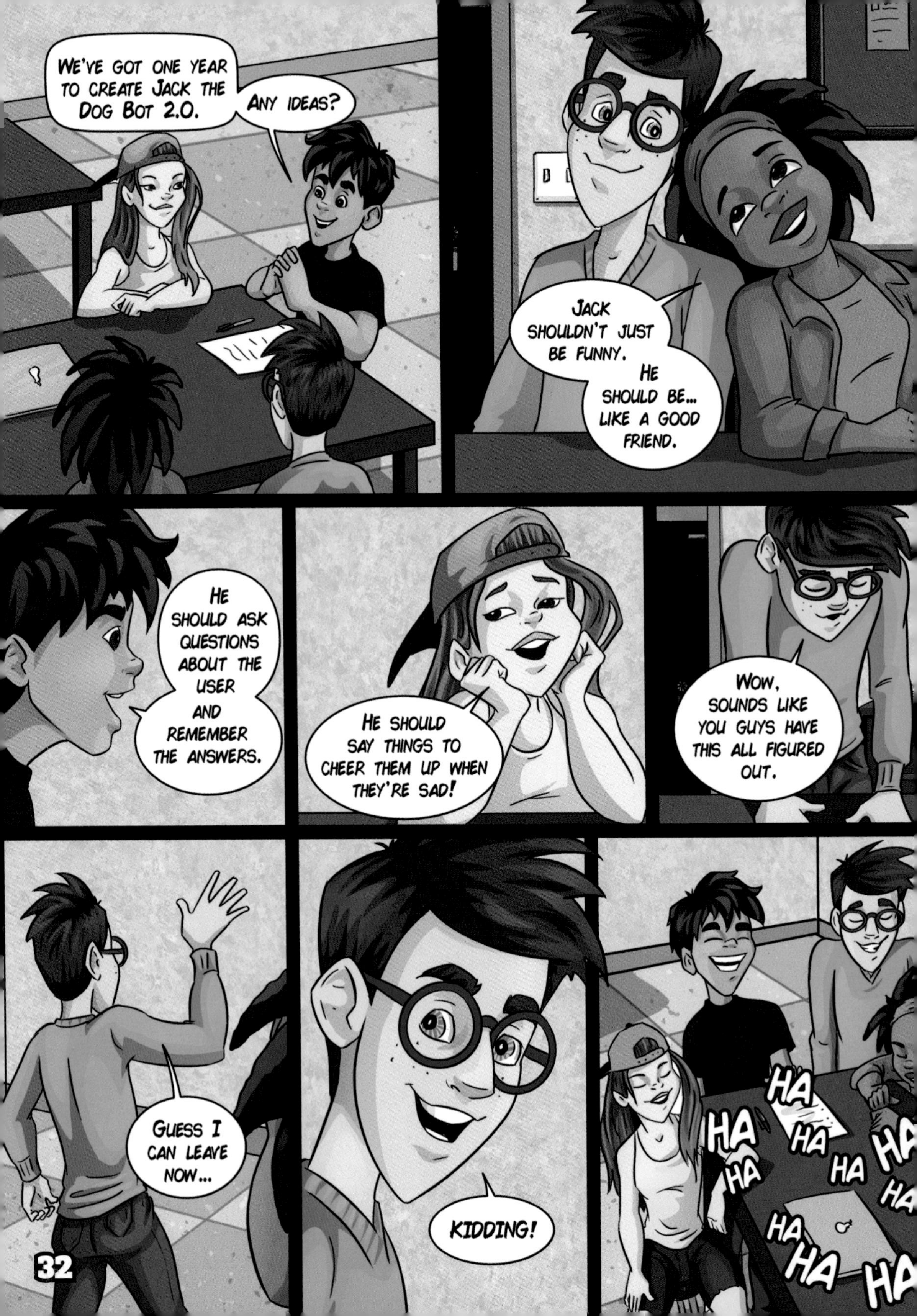
WE'VE GOT ONE YEAR TO CREATE JACK THE DOG BOT 2.0.
ANY IDEAS?
JACK SHOULDN'T JUST BE FUNNY.
HE SHOULD BE... LIKE A GOOD FRIEND.
HE SHOULD ASK QUESTIONS ABOUT THE USER
AND REMEMBER THE ANSWERS.
HE SHOULD SAY THINGS TO CHEER THEM UP WHEN THEY'RE SAD!
WOW, SOUNDS LIKE YOU GUYS HAVE THIS ALL FIGURED OUT.
GUESS I CAN LEAVE NOW...
KIDDING!
HA HA HA HA HA HA HA HA HA HA HA